"Is there a pr
faded comple

She wasn't sure ho... ...
on this as a problem? He already had two children.
How would he feel about having another one—
and with her? What if he demanded sole custody or
didn't want her to have the baby at all? She pressed
her palm to her stomach protectively.

His gaze followed her hand. "Are you ill?"

She shook her head. "It's nothing like that." Cassie
tried to subdue the butterflies in her stomach and
failed. The way they were flapping, they felt more
like giant bats. Maybe she'd acted too hastily.

"Well?" Nick prompted. "Is it good news?"

"We're going to have a baby," she blurted.

For a moment he didn't react at all; he merely
stared.

Suddenly Cassie's elation was replaced by a shiver of
foreboding.

PAMELA TOTH

USA TODAY bestselling author Pamela Toth was born in Wisconsin, but grew up in Seattle, where she attended the University of Washington and majored in art. Now living on the Puget Sound area's east side, she has two daughters, Erika and Melody, and two Siamese cats.

Recently she took a lead from one of her romances and married her high school sweetheart, Frank. They live in a town house within walking distance of a bookstore and an ice-cream shop, two of life's necessities, with a fabulous view of Mount Rainier. When she's not writing, she enjoys traveling with her husband, reading, playing FreeCell on the computer, doing counted cross-stitch and researching new story ideas. She's been an active member of Romance Writers of America since 1982.

Her books have won several awards and they claim regular spots on the Waldenbooks bestselling romance list. She loves hearing from readers and can be reached at P.O. Box 5845, Bellevue, WA 98006. For a personal reply, a stamped, self-addressed envelope is appreciated.

Pamela Toth
The Paternity Test

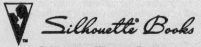

Published by Silhouette Books
America's Publisher of Contemporary Romance

ISBN-13: 978-0-373-36050-5
ISBN-10:   0-373-36050-9

THE PATERNITY TEST

To Elaine Eliason, whose artistry with fabric and glass is exceeded only by the warmth, support and compassion she extends so generously to those lucky enough to have her for a friend.

And to Frank: Forever isn't nearly long enough.

Chapter One

"Eight, nine, ten! Go play in your room till your father gets home."

From his position just inside the massive oak and leaded glass front door, Nick Kincaid could hear the molar-cracking tension in his housekeeper's voice as the other man finished growling out numbers and spoke to the twins, who were four. What had Adam and Amanda done now—and where in Hades was the new nanny Nick had just hired?

After shutting the front door behind him, he crossed the expansive tiled foyer and headed in the direction of Bull's voice. A puddle of soapy water spreading across the floor from the small but elegant powder room halted Nick in his tracks. While he stared in disbelief, the water eddied around his Italian leather shoes.

"Hi, Daddy!" Adam was standing in the doorway

of the powder room with an angelic smile on his face as his sister peeked around him, her blue eyes wide and wary. One stubby finger was curled over her nose and her thumb was jammed securely into her mouth. Behind Nick's children, ex-biker-turned-housekeeper Bull Wylie loomed like a mountain of tattooed granite, his beefy fists planted on his hips, a black leather vest hanging open over his hairy chest.

"About time you got here," Bull grunted before Nick could return Adam's cheerful greeting.

Nick raised one dark eyebrow and did his best to stare down his employee. As usual, his attempt at intimidation failed completely. "I had a meeting," he found himself explaining, instead. "Hi, Adam. Hi, Amanda." He sank down on his haunches, mindful of the bubbles floating around him. "What's going on?"

"We broke the potty," Adam replied.

"We was cleaning it," Amanda added timidly.

Nick wondered why she wasn't more afraid of Bull, all six foot four and three hundred pounds of frowning disapproval, and less fearful of her own father, who squatted harmlessly in front of her and tried to appear more at ease than he felt. Janine had probably filled her little head with horror stories before she'd shipped his children back to him like unwanted parcels. The woman had the maternal instincts of a guppy. No doubt the only reason she'd taken the twins with her when she left him had been to guarantee Nick's continued financial support.

"Where's Mrs. Sweeney?" he asked Bull, who was fingering the Maltese cross that dangled from one ear.

"Gone. Just like you and these young'uns had better be, before I lose my temper and quit, too."

Bull's eyebrows were bunched across his forehead like fat, hairy caterpillars; the small silver hoop that pierced one winked in the late-afternoon light from the leaded windows. Bull threatened to quit at least once every couple of months, but Nick couldn't afford to lose him now. Especially if the latest nanny was indeed gone for good.

"Why'd she leave?" he asked, realizing the water from the bathroom had soaked through the leather of his shoes and was now dampening his socks.

Bull shrugged and the tattooed snake on his biceps writhed. "Dunno. Could have been because she suddenly remembered someplace else she had to be, just the way she said before she took off like a scalded cat. Or it could have had something to do with her spare wig being flushed down the john. What matters is that she's gone, they're here, I got dinner to fix, a mess to clean up and I ain't no plumber."

"This the commode the wig's in?" Nick asked in a carefully neutral voice.

"Yep."

"We was washing it," Adam added helpfully. "But it went down when Mandy flushed, and the water came up, up, up." He motioned with his hand.

Nick gave his son a stern look before turning back to Bull. "Call a plumber," he directed. "Pay whatever it takes to get someone out here today. Don't worry about dinner—I'll take them out." He glanced around. What was he going to do with them? He'd barely gotten used to having kids underfoot. "Get this water cleaned up and then call it a day."

He held out his hands to the twins. "You two

come with me while I change my shoes. And socks,'' he added as he straightened and took a step forward, his shoes squishing noisily.

As soon as the children left the bathroom doorway, each gripping one of Nick's hands like a lifeline, Bull pushed past him.

"My show's on TV," he replied over one shoulder as he lumbered toward his own apartment. "Call the plumber yourself. The mop and pail are in the broom closet off the kitchen." He slapped open the door with the flat of his hand. "If the three of you ain't out of here by the time my show's over, I might do something we'll all regret." He turned to glare at Adam and Amanda until they'd both retreated behind Nick, Amanda's tiny fingers clutching at his pant leg. "And don't come back here without a new nanny."

As Bull disappeared into his private quarters, Nick realized he was opening and closing his mouth like a fish. Frustrated, he clenched his teeth. When had he lost the upper hand? he wondered. Had it been when he'd picked the kids up at the airport three weeks earlier, or two years ago when he'd first hired Bull—right after the biker-turned-minor-league-goon had tried to brain him with a tire iron?

"Daddy," Amanda whispered urgently, standing on tiptoe, "I gotta tinkle."

As a gentle breeze stirred her straight, pale-blond hair, Cassandra Hansen Wainright smoothed one neatly manicured hand along the painted surface of the bench on which she was sitting and stared across the expanse of the park without really seeing anything but a blur of green.

What was she going to do now? Her husband had

been dead for almost a month, killed in a car accident while he was with a girlfriend Cassie hadn't known he'd been seeing. His company was being investigated by the government for reasons she didn't understand, her mother was slipping further away from reality with each passing week and the people Cassie had thought were her friends had begun treating her as if she were the carrier of a social disease.

Feelings of frustration and helplessness welled up inside her as she struggled for control of the angry tears that threatened to spill over. She wanted to confront Robert, to rage at him for betraying their marriage vows and for leaving his life in such an untidy mess for her to deal with. Just this morning her husband's attorney had called to warn her of the impending investigation into Robert's investment business. She'd been too shocked by the news to understand Walter's rambling explanation—something about the SEC and the IRS.

As if that wasn't enough, when she'd cleaned out her late husband's desk, she found a stack of overdue bills, including one from a jeweler for several expensive pieces Cassie had never laid eyes on. Last, but certainly not least, the nursing home had phoned, threatening to move her mother if her seriously overdue account wasn't settled immediately.

Robert had always paid the bills himself, but no doubt he'd gotten too busy for such mundane chores, Cassie thought with a fresh spurt of anger. Apparently, he and Monica Sandford had been on their way to a romantic getaway on the Olympic Peninsula, while Cassie had assumed he was going to an investment symposium in Portland.

Pondering her next move, Cassie buried her aching

head in her hands and closed her eyes against the hurt and disillusionment churning through her, when a noisy sniffle distracted her from her own immediate problems.

"Why do you got your hands over your face? Are you playing hide-and-seek?"

Cassie jerked her head up and stared into the tearful brown eyes of a small boy with yellow hair. He was wearing shorts and a red T-shirt. "Where did you come from?" She glanced around the empty clearing. He was much too little to be in the park alone.

"I came from Paris," he replied. "Why are you crying? Are you lost, too?"

Cassie swiped at her damp cheeks as the child watched with interest. "No, I'm not lost. Are you?"

He nodded solemnly.

"What happened to your parents?" Surely they'd burst from the trees at any moment, relieved to catch up with him.

He shrugged—a curiously adult gesture for one so small. "Mommy's with her boyfriend. Bull's mad and Daddy's with Amanda."

Cassie immediately pictured Amanda as a woman not unlike Robert's little friend—tousled brown hair, short leather skirt and a fondness for nice jewelry. Obviously, the boy's parents were too busy pursuing their own interests to give a thought to the welfare of their child. She glanced around again, but not one hysterical adult popped up from behind the rhododendrons surrounding the clearing.

"Do you remember where you last saw them?" Cassie asked as the little boy climbed up next to her on the park bench and sat down.

He kicked his feet, clad in tiny athletic shoes decorated with a popular logo, and shook his head as tears began running down his cheeks.

"Daddy and Amanda went in the bathroom." He pointed in the general direction of the duck pond and the public rest rooms.

"Together?"

He nodded solemnly.

Cassie's imagination raged. Had his father no shame, no sense of propriety?

"What's your name?" she asked.

"Adam." The little boy's lower lip wobbled, and then, as if he had suddenly realized the seriousness of his plight, he began crying in earnest. "Daddy will be mad. I was s'posed to wait." He rubbed his eyes with his fists. "I want my mommy."

Cassie liked children, but she'd had little practical experience with them. Feeling helpless, she put an arm around his thin shoulders and cuddled him awkwardly.

"It's okay, punkin. Don't cry."

At first he held his small body stiffly upright, but then he collapsed against her with a ragged sigh.

"I'm scared," he whimpered. "Daddy's gonna leave me here."

News reports of child abandonment splashed across Cassie's mind. "I'm sure he's looking for you right now," she replied softly, hoping what she said was true. Poor Adam. His fear tugged at her emotions. She had longed for a baby of her own, and she believed that every child deserved to be wanted by someone.

Blinking away the fresh moisture that gathered in her own eyes, Cassie gave him one last squeeze.

"We'll find your mommy," she promised rashly. Which would be better—to try to locate one of his parents or to find a policeman? Cassie bit her lip as she glanced around. There wasn't a soul in sight.

"Where did you say you thought your daddy was?"

Adam pointed in what she suspected was the opposite direction of the way he'd pointed before.

"Let's see if we can find a policeman to help us," she said, standing up and holding out her hand. Perhaps the child had already been reported missing. If not, surely the officer would know what to do about him.

When Adam wiggled off the bench and put his hand in hers, she gave it a gentle squeeze. "My name is Cassie. Come on, honey, we'll get you unlost as soon as we can."

"You won't leave me?" His fingers clutched at hers.

"No, not till we find your parents." If people like the irresponsible monsters he'd described could be called that, she added silently.

She glanced up and down the gravel path, debating the best route to take. Before she could decide, a man carrying a little girl about Adam's size burst from the bushes. His dark hair was standing on end, as if he'd been running his fingers through it; his tie was unknotted and there were damp patches on his rumpled white dress shirt. His face was flushed and he was frowning.

"Daddy!" Adam exclaimed.

"Adam! What the hell happened to you?"

The man rushed over and set the little girl on the ground, as Cassie felt Adam's hand tremble in hers.

"I'm sorry," the little boy whispered fearfully.

"Don't shout at him!" Cassie cuddled Adam to her protectively. "He was scared to death and you're making it worse!"

"I was a little scared, too." The man glanced at Cassie and his frown faded slightly. "I'm Nick Kincaid."

"I don't care if you're Ronald McDonald," Cassie shot back. "This child's been through enough already without your yelling."

The man dragged in a breath that expanded his wide chest. He was several inches taller than Cassie, with a narrow, attractive face and a strong jaw. Despite his disarray, his air of success reminded her of her late husband, and her hackles rose.

"I only meant that we've met before," the man explained. "Mrs. Wainright, isn't it? Robert was an acquaintance of mine."

A fleeting expression crossed his face as Cassie realized that she did know him.

"I was sorry to hear about his accident," he added in a gentler tone, surprising her.

Distracted, she mumbled her thanks. Before she could demand to know if he had any idea of the danger in which he'd placed his little boy by leaving him unattended, he leaned down and grabbed Adam by the shoulders.

Now that the immediate danger was past, emotion clogged Nick's throat and nearly choked him. Cloaking his fear with annoyance, he gave Adam a slight shake. "Are you okay?" he demanded. "I've been out of my mind with worry."

Trembling, Adam tried to twist away from his

grip. Instantly contrite, Nick let go of the thin shoulders as if he'd been scalded.

"You're just upsetting him. Can't you see he's already frightened?" Pushing her way between them, the Wainright woman glared at Nick, her blue-green eyes snapping with temper, and then she turned her back and began comforting Adam.

Belatedly, Nick realized that was what *he* should have been doing. Her voice was low, almost husky, as she cupped Adam's chin in one delicate hand and spoke to him. Nick wasn't surprised to see how quickly the boy quieted. A little of that kind of attention would have calmed Nick, as well. She was a beautiful woman, slim, with silvery blond hair his fingers itched to glide through.

"You've got a real gift with kids," he muttered as she withdrew a hankie from her jeans pocket and dabbed at a dirty streak on his son's cheek.

"There, there," she soothed, ignoring him. "Everything's going to be okay now."

Nick could only pray she was right, before she fixed him with a disapproving stare.

"I assume these are your children, Mr. Kincaid?"

"Yeah, they're mine." That much, at least, he could be sure of, even if he didn't have a clue how to deal with them. "Please, call me 'Nick.' No doubt you've already met Adam. This is his twin sister."

"Amanda, I assume?"

A peculiar expression crossed her face. As she bent down, the scent of flowers underlaid with something darker, headier, swirled around Nick.

"Hi, I'm Cassie. I bet you're glad to find your brother."

"Real glad," Amanda whispered around her thumb.

Nick realized he was staring at the shadowy cleft framed by the gaping neckline of Cassie's blouse. Reluctantly, he shifted his gaze to his daughter and tried with his usual lack of success to find some resemblance either to himself or to the twins' mother in Amanda's delicate features. The idea that he had actually fathered these two small beings both thrilled and terrified him. Too late, Nick had realized he wasn't cut out to be a parent.

"Thank you for finding my boy," he told Cassie when she straightened. Not only had she found him, she'd defended him from Nick's temper like a cat with her kittens. Compared with Janine's total lack of maternal feeling, he found Cassie's behavior even more impressive.

"I was glad to help." She gave Adam another hug before she let him go.

Careful to keep his voice even, Nick said, "Young man, I thought I asked you to wait right in the rest room while I helped your sister."

Adam's gaze was wary. "Are you gonna spank me?"

Cassie's eyes widened with horror and Nick's own stomach lurched. He had a few questions for Janine when he caught up with her.

"Of course I'm not going to spank you."

As Adam caught the impatience in Nick's voice, his lip began to quiver all over again. Frustrated, Nick swallowed an oath and ground his teeth together. Being a parent was ten times harder than the most complicated financial coup he'd ever pulled off.

"I was very worried when I came out of the bathroom stall with your sister and you were gone," he explained. "I looked everywhere." "Worried" was an understatement. He'd been in a total panic.

Adam's chin wobbled. "I heard a doggie, so I went outside. I wanted to pet it, but I couldn't catch up. Then I found Cassie and she was crying, so I thought she was lost."

Nick glanced at the woman curiously. She was wearing jeans and tennis shoes, her only jewelry a square-cut aquamarine ring whose color exactly matched her eyes. There were faint shadows beneath them, but Nick had heard the rumors surrounding her husband's death. It sounded as though she had plenty of reason to be upset.

Fleetingly, Nick thought of his ex-wife. Would Janine have grieved for him? Unless he'd died broke, he seriously doubted it.

"I wasn't exactly crying," Cassie hedged as color bloomed on her creamy cheeks. "I was just thinking about some things."

"Sad things?" Adam ventured.

Before Nick could reprimand him for the prying question, she looked at Nick and her chin went up. "I suppose so."

He felt a flare of sympathy. If the rumors concerning Robert's business were as persistent as the ones about his unfaithfulness, she must be having money worries, too.

Her problems made Nick's—finding a suitable caretaker for his children—seem trivial, until he remembered Bull's ultimatum. What was he going to do?

As Nick continued to watch Cassie, a possible solution to both her problems and his own popped into his head. It was obvious from the way she'd championed Adam that she cared about children. If she was indeed hurting for money, perhaps they could strike a bargain that would help them both. His gut urged him to go for it, and he always listened to his gut.

"Thanks for taking such good care of my son," he said again, his mind working swiftly. Desperation was a powerful motivator, and he was nothing if not desperate. "Perhaps I could return the favor in some small way."

Cassie frowned. "That's not necessary."

"I have an idea that may be to our mutual advantage," he said, pressing on. "From what I hear, you could use a friend, and I find myself in need of the services of a woman like you."

Her light-blue eyes iced over as splotches of temper flagged her cheeks. "A woman like me?" she echoed.

It would be a great solution for both of them, Nick thought, barely aware of her question.

"Of course. You'd be perfect for what I have in mind." A picture formed in his head of her glancing up from the storybook she was reading the children to give him a smile of welcome.

"And just what did you have in mind?"

The chill in Cassie's voice finally penetrated the bubble of his enthusiasm like a pin pricking a balloon. His smile faltered and he realized he'd phrased the idea badly. Strange, outlining a concept was usually so easy for him. He hadn't been himself since the twins had gotten off the plane. "I was going to offer you a job."

"A job?" Cassie echoed Nick's words as wariness

replaced her disdain. "Doing what?" Nick Kincaid
was an attractive man, if one liked the lean, hungry
type who looked as if he ate competitors for breakfast. The first time she'd met him at a political fund-
raiser, she remembered thinking he reminded her of
a predator. She'd been stalked by more than one of
that ilk since news of her current, dicey financial situation had leaked out.

The first time, at the wake following Robert's funeral, she'd been painfully slow in grasping what one
of his closest friends was suggesting until the man,
gaze dropping to her chest, had spelled it out with a
knowing grin. Furious, Cassie demanded to know if
his wife was aware of his intended act of kindness.
He'd hastily abandoned his suggestion, but since
then, two other acquaintances had hinted at similar
offers.

Was she guilty this time of leaping to conclusions,
or had Nick merely worded his proposition in a new
way?

His glance slid away to the twins, increasing her
suspicion. Was he uncomfortable discussing something this...this sleazy in front of his children?

"I'm desperate for a nanny to watch Adam and
Amanda," he said bluntly. "Someone who'll take
care of them without quitting in a week."

Had he said "nanny"? Cassie couldn't have been
more stunned if he'd said he needed a lion tamer for
his cat.

"I beg your pardon?" She hadn't taken care of
children since she was a teenager eager for spending
money. After her marriage, she and Robert had
wanted a baby, but she hadn't managed to get
pregnant.

"I need a nanny," Nick repeated, his gray eyes flashing with impatience. "You know, a full-time baby-sitter."

"We're not babies," Adam protested.

"Not babies," Amanda echoed in a tiny voice.

Nick's smile was starting to falter. "'Baby-sitter' is just an expression." His dark eyebrows bunched together above his piercing stare like gathering storm clouds. "They need some continuity in their lives. The past three nannies lasted less than a week each. The agency has run out of candidates to send, so I thought you and I might be able to help each other out, that's all." He rubbed his chin. "I didn't mean to give you the wrong impression."

Cassie studied the twins curiously. *Why* had the past three nannies left?

"What about their mother?" she asked. She tried to remember if she knew anything about Mrs. Kincaid, but drew a blank. Cassie hadn't really enjoyed the huge social functions Robert had insisted she attend with him, and now she couldn't picture a wife at Nick's side. Somehow he didn't give off the vibes of a married man. He was too—dynamic, she decided, studying him through her lashes.

To her surprise, he glowered at her question, sending a shiver as chilly as a shard of ice sliding down her spine.

"Their mother—" He paused, glancing at the children, who were watching the exchange with fascination. "Their mother is no longer in the picture."

How had she not heard? "I'm sorry. I didn't realize."

Nick must have read her expression. "No. Oh, no. Janine's in Europe. We're divorced."

The name suddenly brought back the image of a high-maintenance blonde in a long fur, her expression bored. Then Cassie remembered Adam's telling her he'd come from Paris. She couldn't have said why the news that Nick was divorced relaxed some of her tension. He intimidated her. She realized, too, as she suppressed another tremor of nerves, that she couldn't possibly consider working for him in any capacity, no matter how grave her financial situation might become. There was necessity and then there was *survival*.

"I don't know what you've heard about my situation," she told him, "but my husband left a successful business and a sizable estate. I'm not looking for work of any kind."

Nick's disappointment was apparent. "I'm sorry," he said heavily. "I mean, I'm not sorry you aren't destitute. Apparently, what I heard was in error, so I'm sorry I bothered you with my problem."

She ignored her own curiosity. "That's all right. Thank you for your offer. I wish I could be of help— recommend someone—but I haven't had the need for a nanny myself." Robert had been terribly disappointed by her failure to conceive, and so had she. He had a grown son from his first marriage, but he wanted more children. Cassie had undergone several uncomfortable fertility tests, but they'd been inconclusive.

Nick took his wallet from his pocket, extracting a card and thrusting it at her.

"If anything changes," he said, "would you give me a call?"

Automatically, she took the square of heavy, palegray stock and glanced at the bold black lettering.

Nicholas Kincaid, it stated simply, with an address and several other numbers listed on it—phone, fax, pager. As he continued to watch her, his silver eyes unwavering, she tucked the card into her purse without the slightest intent of ever using it.

Cassie looked down at the children. "It was nice to meet you both," she told them. "But now I have to get going." Emma, the woman who ran her house with an iron hand and a soft heart, would worry if Cassie was late for dinner. She wondered if the household staff had heard the rumors about the investigation. If so, they must be concerned. Perhaps she'd better say something to them. But what?

After the twins had bade her goodbye and Adam gave her a hug, she returned her attention to their father and held out her hand, although she would rather not touch him again. Heat and energy emanated from him like rays from a microwave—invisible, but having the potential to inflict serious damage. She didn't understand why, but she suspected he could be very dangerous, indeed.

"Thank you again for rescuing Adam."

He held her hand a moment too long and then released it when she was about to pull free.

"Call me if there's anything at all I can do. I mean it. Or if you change your mind about the position."

Cassie ignored the mild tingling in her fingers. "I won't change my mind." She didn't add that he must be desperate, to trust his children to someone without even checking references.

Nick was thinking the same thing as he watched her walk away, her trim hips swinging slightly. Even though he'd met her before, he knew very little about her except that she was Robert Wainright's second wife, that more than a few years had separated them and, according to the rumor mill he usually ignored, she'd apparently been no more eager to ruin her figure or tie herself down with children than had been his own wife. If she was so indifferent, why had she leaped to Adam's defense?

Still, having her around would certainly be a distraction. Perhaps Nick was lucky she'd turned down his offer after all, even if it did mean facing Bull without reinforcements.

When Janine had first announced her pregnancy, she'd been understandably upset. Although Nick hadn't considered marrying her before that, he'd wanted a family someday. She was attractive, seemingly insatiable in bed, and had the background to be a good hostess. It was only after the wedding that her true colors began to appear. The last thing he needed in his life right now was another blonde with the potential to make him think with his hormones instead of his brain.

"Can we get ice cream?" Adam asked, tugging at Nick's hand.

The little boy's request dragged him back to reality. He glanced at his watch. First, he'd better call one of the other agencies from his car phone. If he couldn't bring back a nanny, as Bull had stipulated, at least he could try to line one up for the next day.

"Sure," he drawled. "If you're quiet while I make a call, we'll have hot dogs, with ice cream for dessert. How would that be?"

"Of course, Isobel, I understand perfectly. I'll talk to you soon." Cassie set down the receiver and blinked back tears of frustration and humiliation. It was amazing how quickly her friends were deserting her, now that word of the investigation into Robert's company had gotten around.

Friends, indeed. Robert's friends, she amended silently. People who'd never really accepted into their ranks the naive salesclerk he'd married and who now were obviously only too eager to cut her from their guest lists, as well, as Isobel Lindstrom had just done with a transparent excuse.

Cassie squared her shoulders and pushed away from the rolltop desk of teak and brass.

"Trouble?" asked Emma as she hovered nearby, an unused feather duster in one hand. Emma had been with Robert for a number of years when Cassie had come to the house as a new and nervous bride. For some reason of her own, Emma had welcomed her warmly. Now Cassie liked to think they were more than employer and employee. They'd become friends. Unlike Isobel, real friends.

"Another cancellation of an invitation I didn't care about," Cassie replied with a deliberately unconcerned gesture.

Emma frowned and pursed her lips. "Don't mind them," she said. "They aren't worth the effort."

Cassie couldn't help but smile at the older woman's expression. She was as protective as Cassie's own mother had once been.

"I'm getting used to it," she replied. More troublesome was the investigation. What would happen to Robert's estate if irregularities were found? Would there be a fine? Would the resulting scandal hurt his business?

Cassie needed to talk with Miles, Robert's adult son, who had been running the company since his father's death. There were questions she wanted to ask.

Before Emma could say anything more, the phone on the desk rang again.

"I'll get it," Cassie said as she reached for the receiver. Her shoulders stiffened with tension when she recognized the voice of the administrator of the nursing home where Cassie's mother was a patient. "Is Mom okay?" she asked, cutting through the polite greeting.

"Mrs. Hansen's health hasn't changed," Mrs. Cathcart replied. "She has her good days. It's a financial matter I've called to discuss." She cleared her throat. "I'm afraid the check you sent to bring your account up-to-date has been returned by your bank. Since the account's so far in arrears, I wanted to bring the matter to your personal attention."

Embarrassed, Cassie promised to straighten out the problem immediately with the bank and call Mrs. Cathcart back.

"Thank you, dear. Your mother is comfortable here and we wouldn't want to upset her routine by having to relocate her at this point in her treatment."

Her stomach knotting at the implied threat, Cassie broke the connection, then looked up the number for the bank. Although her mother had Alzheimer's, there were times she was perfectly lucid. It had taken quite a while for her to accept her surroundings and Cassie hated the idea of having to move her again and put her through another difficult period of adjustment. Besides, Woodlake was the finest facility of its kind in the Bellevue area, as well as being convenient to the house.

When Cassie finally got through the bank's voice

mail and made contact with a customer representative, she outlined the problem. To her irritation, as soon as the woman brought up Cassie's account, she was put back on hold.

Finally, a man's disembodied voice came on the line.

"I'm sorry to tell you this, Mrs. Wainwright," he said in an expressionless tone, "but we cannot cover the check in question, nor can we allow any activity in any of your accounts at this time."

"What do you mean?" Cassie demanded, her fingers tightening on the receiver. "Are you telling me I'm overdrawn? Let me assure you, that isn't possible." Obviously, some gigantic computer error had been made. They'd owe her a whopping apology once it was straightened out. She might even take her business elsewhere.

"No, Mrs. Wainwright, there's a healthy balance in the account in question," he replied. "We just can't touch it, and neither can you. The IRS has ordered that your financial assets be frozen until further notice. I'm so sorry."

Chapter Two

"You just can't get anywhere with those banker types," Emma grumbled as she sliced up a kiwi and added it to the fruit plate she'd been pestering Cassie to eat. "They think they know everything." Emma's brown eyes were like raisins in her lined face. With her glasses suspended from a chain around her neck, her neat, dark blouse and matching straight skirt and her sensible shoes, she could have passed for a high-school teacher instead of a long-time employee who spoke her mind with easy familiarity.

There was no way Cassie could have kept the news about the IRS's freezing her bank accounts from Emma. She had needed to confide in someone, and the housekeeper was the closest thing to family Cassie had since her own mother's Alzheimer's had become so advanced. Even on Adele Hansen's good days, Cassie was unwilling to worry her.

"The man at the bank didn't have a choice," she explained now as she selected a fresh strawberry and absently popped it into her mouth.

Pursing her thin lips, Emma made a sound of disbelief. "You've been through enough in the past few weeks without this happening." Cassie knew she wasn't referring only to Robert's death. Emma had been well aware of the deterioration of their marriage and she might have suspected his adultery, as well. Not much got past her. Had Cassie been the only one too blind to see what was going on under her nose?

She hadn't told Emma about Nick Kincaid's job offer. It was too ridiculous to mention, and no doubt he'd found someone else to care for his children by now. As cute as the twins were, there must be some reason he'd had so much trouble keeping nannies that he'd been desperate enough to offer the job to her.

"You have to eat something," Emma scolded.

The admonishment brought Cassie's attention sharply back to the present. The fruit plate was now sitting in front of her on the granite-covered eating bar and Emma was watching her with hands planted on her spare hips.

"Got any idea what you're going to do?" Emma asked as Cassie eyed the fruit with little interest.

"I'll eat," Cassie said, resigned.

"No, girl, I mean about your financial plight." The housekeeper rolled her eyes. The only time she'd bothered to stand on ceremony was around Cassie's husband. He'd insisted on it.

Cassie knew the older woman wasn't worried about her own paycheck. She'd saved enough over the years that she could retire whenever she wanted, but she'd told Cassie on more than one occasion that she was afraid she'd die in her sleep if she quit working.

"I called Walter Beck," Cassie replied, mentioning the attorney who had handled Robert's legal affairs for the past twenty years.

Emma snorted as she rinsed off the paring knife and cutting board. "The man's a snake."

Emma had no use for attorneys. Doctors, accountants and politicians were also on her blacklist, and Cassie suspected the entire workforce of the Internal Revenue Service had recently joined them, as well.

"Walter didn't have any idea where I could get the money to tide us over," Cassie continued as if Emma hadn't spoken. She wondered what Emma would think of Nick Kincaid. Her own husband had been a bus driver who'd died years ago, before Emma had come to work for Robert. Cassie had long suspected Emma had taken to her so readily because she'd been a salesclerk before her marriage, with roots as ordinary as Emma's own.

"What about a mortgage on this mausoleum?" The housekeeper gestured at their surroundings with the paring knife. Robert had paid cash for the house years earlier when he'd made his first big financial killing. Except for the master suite, which had been redecorated when he married Cassie, the interior still bore the stamp of his first wife's impeccable taste. Even though most of the furnishings were more ornate than Cassie liked, she'd never had the confidence to insist on changes. Now, when she could least afford it, she felt like redoing the house from top to bottom.

Regretfully, she shook her head. "I thought of refinancing, but Robert mortgaged the house to the hilt just over a year ago. Apparently, he poured all the money into the business." Vaguely, she remembered that he'd asked her to sign some papers at the time, papers he'd assured her she didn't need to read. Now she was embarrassed by her own naïveté. "Besides," she added, "no one would lend us a dime against collateral that might be forfeited to the government."

Emma leaned over and patted Cassie's hand. "That isn't going to happen. Meanwhile, we'll think of something."

Cassie rolled a seedless grape around on her plate. Several years ago, her husband had confided that he always kept a supply of cash hidden in the library for emergencies. After the funeral she'd located his cache, but there hadn't been nearly as much as she had hoped. At one time in her life the small stack of bills would have seemed like a fortune; now it was barely enough to cover the immediate expenses for another couple of weeks. Perhaps Robert had depleted his reserves for an emergency of his own, such as a new bauble for Monica.

"I went to see Miles this afternoon," Cassie admitted, losing interest in the grape. Her husband's only child, a year older than Cassie, Miles had already graduated from college and had been working at RWC when she'd married his father six years ago. Now he had his hands full keeping the company afloat in the light of its recent difficulties.

"I wish he'd have come to dinner when you invited him," Emma replied. Miles had begged off, using the pressures at work as his excuse. "How is he?"

Cassie know the older woman was fond of Robert's son. After his mother's death, Emma had practically raised him while Robert had spent long hours at the office, building his business empire.

"He's doing his best to hold things together." Cassie twirled a strand of her hair and remembered the regret on Miles's face when she'd reluctantly asked for a loan. "Of course, his assets are frozen, too." She didn't add that he'd seemed genuinely concerned. She didn't want to admit, even to Emma, that she'd been desperate enough to ask him for money.

For a fleeting moment, the image of Nick Kincaid muscled its way into Cassie's consciousness. Ruthless, handsome and sophisticated, he could have been a younger version of her husband. That must be why she thought of him now, because he and Robert were so much alike—intelligent, ambitious and used to getting their own way.

She might not have been smart enough, at twenty-three, to see through Robert's charm to the ruthlessness behind it, but at least she'd managed so far to ignore her unwelcome attraction toward Nick.

In fact, she wasn't sure why she was even thinking about him now. Hadn't she learned her lesson?

"I feel sorry for Miles, having to take on all these business problems," Emma murmured, "but he's his father's son. He'll manage."

Cassie knew how reluctant Robert had been to give up any control, to delegate even to his heir. Of course, Robert could have had no idea that he'd be dead at fifty-one. Was Miles truly prepared to take over?

She waited to experience some emotion besides bitter anger and a deep sense of betrayal toward her late husband—perhaps a remnant of the love she'd felt at the beginning or at least some grief over his untimely death. But her only regret was that she wasn't able to confront him with her feelings.

Her affection toward him had died long ago, she realized now, the victim of his loss of interest in her when she'd failed to become pregnant. Despite her own efforts to return their relationship to a warmer footing, she knew now that she and Robert had merely been going through the motions.

A sob rose in Cassie's throat, but she refused to let it escape. Maxmillian, Robert's dog, kept his vigil in the arched doorway, his head on his paws and his worried brown eyes staring at Cassie expectantly. How sad that the aging boxer, his once black muzzle now as grizzled as an old man's whiskers and his forehead lined with wrinkles, mourned Robert more deeply than his wife did.

"Poor Max," she murmured.

At the sound of his name, the dog lifted his head, ears twitching, and his gaze swiveled to the back door. When it remained solidly closed, he dropped his head back to his paws and squeezed his eyes shut.

Cassie sighed. "Of course Miles will manage," she reassured Emma. "He has his father's head for business." He had to succeed in holding the company together—their financial futures depended on it, as did Cassie's mother's security. "Meanwhile, I guess I'd better start looking for a job."

"A job!" Emma echoed. "Surely you aren't that desperate."

To her utter humiliation, Cassie felt her eyes fill with tears. Weepy women irritated her. Blinking away the moisture, she admitted part of the truth.

"The wolf's getting closer to the door. Robert had

been letting the bills slide. I did my best to bring them up-to-date, but there's not much money left over. Walter warned me the investigation might drag on for months, and the nursing home is threatening to have Mom moved.''

Cassie wished she could bring her mother home, but she had tried that once and it hadn't worked out. When lucid, Cassie's mother had been uncomfortable in the ostentatious surroundings; when not, she'd put herself in danger on more than one occasion. The best place for her now was Woodlake.

Emma frowned thoughtfully. ''I have some money put aside—''

Cassie gave the other woman a quick hug and then she shook her head. ''Thanks, but you'll need that for your retirement.''

Emma was frowning. ''I told you I'm never going to retire. I'd rather die in harness.''

The words made Cassie shiver. ''I still can't take your money.'' She would sling hash at a truck stop first. And she might have to do just that; she was running out of options and panic was starting to pound behind her eyes with the discordant beat of a drum.

''Well, if you won't let me help, at least you won't have to worry about my salary until this is settled.''

''I can't do that,'' Cassie murmured as her throat tightened with emotion.

Emma's expression was set into stubborn lines. ''You don't have a choice.''

''There's a call for you, Mr. Kincaid.''

Nick's secretary's voice, pleasantly husky, wafted

from the intercom on his desk to permeate his office like wood smoke.

"It's Mr. Wylie."

Again? With a premonition of disaster, Nick picked up the receiver, only to slam it back down moments later. Swearing, he grabbed his suit jacket and headed out the door of his office. Exasperation churned in his gut like leftover chili.

"I'll be gone the rest of the day," he told his startled secretary as he stalked past her desk. "I have to pick up the twins."

"But you have a meeting with—"

"Cancel it, Opal." He could barely hold back a snarl of pure frustration. The day-care center had just been closed because of an epidemic—of head lice!

After he'd run into Cassie Wainright at the park, Nick had struck out in finding an available nanny. In desperation, he'd hired a teenager. A few days later, she'd quit to work in a boutique at the mall and he'd been reduced to leaving the twins at a day-care center near his office.

Bull's voice on the phone had been totally without expression when he reminded Nick to stop by the drugstore and pick up some special shampoo, right before he mentioned that *he* was heading for a hotel and putting his room on Nick's tab.

Damn. As Nick drove his Mercedes from the parking garage below his building, he could still remember the humiliation of being singled out and sent home by the school nurse. His mother had washed every article of their clothes and bedding in hot water after nearly scrubbing his scalp raw.

He was afraid to think what the next crisis might be, but he knew one thing for sure. No way was he exposing his children to another public day-care center anytime soon. Before he did that, he'd stay home with them himself.

By the time Nick had picked up Adam and Amanda, tried to assure them they'd done nothing wrong and taken them home to wash their hair, strip their beds and run several loads of laundry while he fed them a dinner of macaroni and cheese from a box, he was exhausted and they were whiny and sullen. How did single mothers cope? Longing for something simple to deal with, like a hostile takeover, he popped a tape in the VCR and settled them in front of a movie about a talking pig while he tried to figure out what to do next.

After a half hour of pacing and wasted phone calls, Nick got to his feet and unrolled the shirt sleeves he'd rolled up at bath time. From down the hall, he could hear high-pitched laughter. The tension in his shoulders eased slightly; he'd learned the hard way it was when all was quiet that he had to worry the most.

As a temporary diversion the television had its moments, but he needed more than a television for the next day. He needed a human being with a heart and some common sense to watch his kids. Scratching his jaw absently, Nick realized he'd nearly run out of choices.

Twenty minutes later he parked his car on a quiet, tree-lined cul de sac in an exclusive neighborhood east of Lake Sammamish and unfastened his children from their car seats.

"Are those Christmas trees?" Adam tilted back his blond head to gape at the tall Douglas firs as he tugged on Nick's hand.

"I guess they are," Nick responded absently.

"Why don't they have lights and things?"

"Because it's not Christmas, silly," Amanda told her brother as the three of them stopped to look through an open gate at an imposing Spanish-style house.

In the gathering twilight its white stucco walls glowed softly beneath a red tiled roof. Curling black wrought-iron planters spilling over with bright-yellow flowers trimmed its tall windows. In the courtyard a fountain splashed softly, and warm, golden light streamed from ornate lanterns hung from heavy chains on either side of the elaborately carved double front doors.

"Is this a hotel?" Adam asked.

"This is a house. It belongs to a friend of ours." Nick hoped he wasn't stretching the truth too far. Clinging to his other hand, Amanda followed him across the driveway, but she hung back when he tried guiding her up the brick steps.

"I want to go home now," she said.

Feeling awkward, Nick squatted beside her. "Do you remember the lady you met at the park?" he asked, swallowing his impatience.

She nodded, her thumb in her mouth. Her curling brown hair danced around her small, pale face. "Cassie. She was nice."

"She lives here?" Adam peered around with new interest. "Wow. She must be rich."

His remark made Nick smile. It must be the wrought iron or the tiled roof that impressed Adam so much.

Nick wondered if he should have called first, but he had learned that a surprise attack sometimes worked best. Besides, he was tired, he was desperate and he had no idea what he'd do if she turned him down again. With a sigh and a silent prayer, he rose and led the twins to the front door. Letting go of Adam's hand, Nick rang the bell.

From inside the house, a dog started barking.

"I'm scared," Amanda whimpered.

"It's okay." Nick didn't expect Cassie to answer the door herself. When she did, a jolt of reaction went through him. Behind her stood a fierce-looking dog with its gaze riveted on Nick's throat. The twins crowded behind him.

"Do you remember us?" he asked Cassie when she held the door wide and stared up at him with a perplexed expression.

He'd forgotten how pretty she was, or maybe he hadn't really noticed the other day. His mind had been on Adam at the time. Now, despite her companion's growl, he couldn't help but stare into her blue-green eyes, tilted up at the corners. In the soft light of early evening, the irises appeared darker than had been his first impression.

"Of course I remember you."

Her silvery blond hair was gathered into a big clip, with strands sticking up at strange angles, making her look like a teenager—and making Nick feel like an aging lecher. She was wearing a straight tan skirt that ended above her knees and a sleeveless white silk shirt, but her feet were bare. Nick almost grinned when he noticed that her toenails were painted a soft pink.

Snapping her fingers, Cassie silenced her dog. With obvious reluctance it retreated, and then she stepped through the doorway.

"Adam, Amanda, how have you been?" she asked, smiling.

"Hi, Cassie," Adam replied, stepping forward. "We got bugs in our hair, so Daddy got us from day care and now we got nowhere to go, so we're here."

Cassie's smile faded and she looked up at Nick for clarification. Fascinated, he stared at her full lips, naked, soft, as pink as her toenails. When she pressed her lips together, the spell was broken and he cleared his throat.

"Perhaps you'd better let me tell her, sport." Nick could feel the heat of embarrassment climb his cheeks. He'd faced a roomful of angry stockholders with less trepidation.

"Bugs?" Cassie echoed, eyes wary.

He sighed and glanced around as a man on a bike made a lazy U-turn in the cul de sac. In a nearby yard, an older woman called to a small scruff of a mutt.

"It's a long story," Nick said.

Cassie took his hint and stepped back into the entry, bare feet soundless on the flagstone floor.

"Perhaps you'd better come inside." The dog was sitting several feet away, his unwavering attention on Nick. "Don't worry about Max," she added. "He's really very friendly."

"Does he bite?" Adam asked.

"Only hot dogs and burglars," she replied, making him giggle.

The sound relieved a little of Cassie's worry. Adam appeared to be a happy child, not one who had reason to fear his father. Perhaps Nick's temper the other day had been an isolated incident. She certainly hoped so.

As she led him and the children through the archway into the formal living room, she could feel Nick's gaze. She wished he hadn't caught her with her face and feet bare, her hair anchored with a plastic clip.

Earlier, Emma had gone off to read a mystery in her room. Cassie had been looking through the papers in Robert's office again with the distant hope of finding something, anything, that might give her a solution to the problems closing in on her.

Instead, Nick Kincaid was here to fuel her adolescent fantasies. Why had he come?

"Please, sit down." She gestured toward the oversized leather sectional as she heard Maxmillian's toenails clicking against the floor tiles. He stood watch in the doorway.

"Nice doggie," Adam said as he sat next to Nick.

His stump of a tail wagging, Max glanced at Cassie, but she shook her head. With a noisy sigh, he flopped to the floor.

"Can I get you anything?" Cassie asked her guests.

Adam opened his mouth, but Nick forestalled him with a glance. "No, thanks. We're here because their day care closed unexpectedly and I'm desperate. Have you had the chance to reconsider my offer?"

His dark eyebrows rose above eyes that were shadowed with fatigue. His mouth, too, was bracketed with lines that appeared deeper than she remembered, and the beginnings of a beard darkened his strong jaw.

Beside him, Adam whispered to his sister as he pointed at the large saltwater aquarium set into the wall. Orange-and-white clown fish darted around a piece of coral, and a purple sea anemone waved tentacles as graceful as a hula dancer's hands.

"I'm sorry," she told Nick, ignoring the quick pinch of her conscience. "I really haven't thought about it. I assumed you'd found someone else." What she'd really assumed was that his suggestion had been an impulse he'd since regretted. "Why did the day-care center close?"

Nick flushed. "Head lice. They're contagious, but you don't need to worry. These two have been properly fumigated."

"Daddy scrubbed us good," Adam commented. "And he said some bad words. Can we look at the fish?"

"Sure." Cassie rose from the chair she'd been perched on with one foot tucked beneath her, and crossed to the window to put some distance between her and Nick as the children went over to the tank.

"I didn't realize you were serious about the job offer," she told him.

He came over beside her as Max remained watchful. "More so than ever, I'm afraid. My situation has gotten critical." Nick's gaze softened. "What about you? I've heard the rumors that your late husband's company is being investigated. Has anything been resolved?"

For a moment, she was tempted to lie. "No," she found herself admitting, instead. "There's been no word about the investigation yet." Still, his offer was ludicrous. A nanny's wages wouldn't go very far in bailing her out of her current situation. Besides, she couldn't see herself working for him, desperate though she might be. She'd read a lot of books about babies and children, so she wasn't a complete novice, but something about him put her survival instincts on red alert. And Lord knows, when it came to men and their character, her judgment wasn't all that reliable.

"I'm sorry," she said, taking another tiny step back, "but I really can't help you."

His frown deepened and he gave the twins a harried glance. "Adam, take your mouth off the glass. You're making a mess."

"But the fish is blowing me kisses," he protested.

Nick's voice was stern. "You heard me."

"I'm sure he won't hurt anything," Cassie murmured.

Nick shrugged, dividing his attention between her and his children. "Look, I heard your assets have been frozen. You're in a jam and so am I. Just say yes."

Parting the lace curtains, Cassie stared through the leaded glass to the patio on the side of the house. Bright-yellow marigolds, red petunias and deep-blue lobelia spilled from a row of terra cotta pots surrounding a pool filled with carp.

The peaceful setting usually calmed her; tonight it failed to do so. Her mother could be turned out into the street. Cassie could lose this house, and right now the only apparent solution was to care for someone else's children, when all she'd wanted from life was a family of her own. How had everything gotten so out of control?

"Cassie?"

Nick spoke from directly behind her, his breath on her neck. It felt as if the tiny hairs there were standing straight up.

"I'm desperate enough for you to name your price," he coaxed.

She remembered the quote "Beware a desperate man; he has nothing to lose." Only conscious effort kept her from shivering. Her gaze stayed riveted on the outdoor pool and she thought of her mother, who had loved feeding the colorful fish whenever she came to visit. The last time, imprisoned in a world of her own, she had shown no interest in them.

"Dammit, Adam, I told you to stop that!" Nick exclaimed.

With a guilty start, the little boy stepped back from the fish tank. Amanda paled at her father's irritated tone.

Cassie's heart ached for all of them. How could she refuse to help? Taking a deep breath, she made a sudden decision she might very well live to regret.

She knew the nursing home fee by heart. "Perhaps I do have a price." Digging her fingernails into her palms, she named the figure aloud.

Except for a slight narrowing of his eyes, Nick kept his face blank. "Is that a quarterly amount?" he asked dryly.

Heat raced up Cassie's cheeks, but she kept her gaze steady on his. "Monthly," she replied, feeling guilty for taking advantage of his situation. Surely he would laugh in her face.

When he turned away, she assumed he was going to grab his kids and go. Part of her regretted the impression he must have of her as a greedy opportunist, but she had no choice. Instead, he merely gazed at the twins, who were looking at Robert's collection of antique snuff boxes in the tall étagère. Amanda's nose was pressed to the curved glass door and her brother was examining the catch with busy fingers.

"Adam," Nick said in a warning voice.

The little boy stiffened and his hands went into his pockets.

"Thank you."

"They're just testing you," Cassie remarked.

Nick turned back to her, a desperate light in his eye. "That's a test I'm genetically programmed to fail," he replied, confusing her. "But I'll pay what you ask on one condition."

She swallowed the impulse to rescind her offer and braced herself for some outrageous demand, instead. "What's your condition?" She could still say no, she reasoned. He couldn't force her to take the job.

"Sign a six-month contract."

"Why?" she asked warily. Why *did* he have so much trouble keeping nannies?

He shrugged. "The kids need a little continuity in their lives, someone to stick around for a while. So far, the turnover has been rather high, so I need a guarantee that you won't bail out the moment your finances get untangled."

Guilt pricked at her. "I wouldn't do that." Would her finances be untangled in half a year? What if the government took everything?

Nick appeared skeptical. "It's only for six months."

"I guess that seems reasonable," she agreed reluctantly. "But maybe you'd better tell me what happened to the other nannies."

The hard line of his mouth relaxed slightly. "They're not buried in the basement, if that's what you're thinking."

Cassie flushed. How could she admit that she'd wondered if he'd made unwelcome overtures or expected from the others more than a nanny's usual duties? Were those suspicions any less insulting than what he'd suggested?

"Adam and Amanda haven't tied anyone up or shaved their heads yet." Thoughtfully, he rubbed his jaw. "They did drown one woman's wig, though."

Cassie might have smiled, but she was too busy ignoring the little warning buzzers going off inside her, the ones screaming that this whole idea was insane and she'd be better off working as a cashier at Shop and Save.

"For the most part, the turnover has been the result of an unfortunate series of coincidences," he continued.

Cassie pursed her lips consideringly. Could sexual harassment be considered an unfortunate coincidence? Did she honestly think a man who looked like Nick and had money, too, would ever be desperate enough to stoop to harassing nannies?

"I don't know what to think," she admitted.

Nick grinned wickedly, making her blink in surprise. He looked like a swashbuckling pirate. All he needed was an earring and an eye patch, and a dagger clamped between his teeth.

"For what I'm paying you, it shouldn't really matter if they do tie you up and shave your head," he drawled. Automatically, her hand went to her hair, as he chuckled softly. "It's such pretty hair, too."

He looked over at the children. "Their mother shipped them back to me less than a month ago, with no explanation and damned little warning. I hear she has a new boyfriend and the kids cramped her style."

His expression had turned forbidding, and Cassie realized he was no man to cross.

"I'm sure they'll adjust, with a little time." Although she couldn't help but feel sorry for them all, she tried to sound reassuring.

"Come and help them to do that."

Somehow, he made it sound like an adventure.

She wondered how much experience with children *he* had, but could think of no way to ask. Instead, she glanced at Adam, who was extending a hand to Max. The dog's tail wagged uncertainly. Right now the twins looked like little angels.

Cassie could feel the coiled tension in Nick as he watched them. "Max is very good with children," she told him. "They're totally safe with him."

Max sniffed Adam's fingers and then ducked his head invitingly. Instantly, both children began petting him and talking to him. Adam even pulled at the loose skin of his jowls.

"His skin's too big," he observed, making Amanda giggle.

Max responded by washing her face with his tongue.

"What about my hours and duties?" Cassie asked Nick as some of the tension left his wide shoulders. "I have no experience at this. I don't even know what to ask. Do I clean your house, fix their meals? What about the laundry?" At least she could cook, even though Emma hardly ever allowed her in her own kitchen.

"I have a housekeeper who does all that," he replied, frowning. "Your sole responsibility will be the children."

Cassie was relieved to hear there was another woman in his employ. Would she guard her domain jealously or would the two of them get along?

"What about hours and days off?" She was pleased with herself for coming up with the businesslike inquiry.

Nick pursed his lips and thought for a moment. "You'll be responsible for getting the kids up, seeing that they're fed and taking care of them while I'm at work. I leave early and I often get stuck late, so your hours will have to be flexible, but I'll make sure you have at least one day a weekend off, two if possible. How's that?"

Cassie thought of the salary she'd demanded and had the grace to flush. "That sounds fair," she murmured, dropping her gaze. This whole conversation was moving too fast for her. She needed time to mull over the offer. "I'll need a couple of days to decide—" she began.

He ran a hand through his dark hair and she noticed for the first time the sprinkling of gray.

"I don't have a couple of days. I have a meeting in the morning that I can't postpone and several important business trips I've been putting off for too long as it is."

Cassie wondered about the housekeeper. Perhaps the woman was too busy or just too old to take on two active preschoolers.

"This is a one-time offer and it expires tonight," Nick added. "If you accept, you start in the morning."

One glance at his steady gaze and Cassie could see he wasn't bluffing. She'd hate to face him over a negotiating table. As desperate as he was, if she procrastinated, he'd withdraw the offer. An offer, she hated admitting, even silently, that she couldn't afford to refuse.

To give herself a moment to think, she turned again to the window and the tranquil pool of fish. Her mother needed her and she needed the money he was willing to pay. There was no other choice, so why did she hesitate?

Cassie glanced at the twins. Could she make a difference in their lives? Help them through a rough time? Resolutely, she faced Nick.

"I'll do it."

For a moment, his face sharpened and she got a glimpse of the ruthless businessman who had built a financial empire far greater than Robert's.

"Good," he said on an exhaled breath. From his pocket he withdrew a folded paper and a pen trimmed in gold. "I prepared a contract, just in case you agreed. I'll fill in the details and we can both sign it."

A shiver went through her as she wondered just how sure of his persuasive powers and her eventual capitulation he'd been, but she had herself back under control by the time he'd penned in the salary amount and handed her the paper.

It was a straightforward agreement that she would work as a nanny to his children for six months from the date of signing. Willing her hand to remain steady, Cassie took the pen he held out and signed her name below his.

"Be there at seven tomorrow morning," Nick told her when she'd handed him back the contract. "I'll introduce you to my housekeeper and you can unpack before your day officially starts. If you don't have time to bring everything tomorrow, I'll send Bull over to get the rest later."

Bull? "Unpack?" she asked. "What do you mean? I'll be coming back here tomorrow night."

Nick narrowed his eyes as he refolded the paper and slipped it into his pocket. "Oh, no, you won't. Didn't I mention it? You'll be living in."

Chapter Three

"Hello, little lady. A bit early to be out peddling makeup or whatever you've got in your bag of goodies, isn't it?"

Disconcerted, Cassie gaped at the hairy behemoth who was eyeing her black leather tote bag with a disdainful smirk. Despite her misgivings about living in at Nick's house, she'd seen the wisdom of it when he'd explained last evening how unpredictable his hours tended to be. Now she stepped back to look at the brass numbers beside the tall double front doors of this imposing mansion that made her own house look like a tract home.

According to the exclusive Medina address, she had the right place.

"I'm sorry," she told the man guarding the entry. "I'm looking for the Kincaid residence."

"You found it."

"Bull, was that the doorbell?" Nick shouted from the depths of the house. "I didn't have time to tell you, but—"

He appeared behind the other man, an exasperated expression on his lean face as he shrugged into a charcoal gray suit jacket. A silk tie in a subtle shade of purple dangled from the neck of his striped shirt and he held an electric razor in one hand.

Nick saw Cassie and grimaced.

"I meant to answer the door myself," he said, "but Adam couldn't find one shoe and then Amanda needed help with her buttons." He edged past the human bulkhead blocking the doorway. "If you'd gotten here sooner—"

Cassie wasn't about to admit that she'd become lost on the way. The man she could have sworn Nick had addressed as "Bull" seemed to swell up even bigger.

"Ya wanna tell me what's going on?" he asked in a gravelly voice.

Nick ignored the interruption. "Cassie," he said with a crooked grin, "this is my housekeeper, Bull Wylie. Bull, the new nanny, Cassie Wainright. Perhaps you'd like to move aside so she can come in."

Ignoring his boss's suggestion, Bull eyed Cassie for a long moment, while she tried not to fidget. Then he grinned, revealing a gaping hole where one front tooth should have been.

"Pleased to meetcha."

He extended a paw the size of a dinner plate. Barely hesitating, Cassie laid her hand across his wide palm. "It's nice meeting you, too." It had never occurred to her to ask Nick if his housekeeper was a woman. Now her vision of a feminine ally to bond with over afternoon tea went the way of the dime phone call.

Bull's palm was calloused, but the clasp of his thick fingers was surprisingly gentle.

"Sorry about the makeup-lady crack," he said in a voice that seemed to rumble up from somewhere deep in his torso, bare except for a leather vest that hung open and several silver chains that gleamed dully from the thicket of curly brown chest hair. "I just got here myself."

Cassie wondered why *he* didn't have to live in. Then she remembered that she'd left Max in the car, and was about to retrieve him, when Adam called out a greeting.

"Cassie! You're here—you're here!" He peered between the railings that fronted the landing at the top of the curving staircase. "Mandy, Cassie's here."

Adam rushed headlong down the stairs, slowing marginally when Nick cautioned him, and wormed his way past Bull, who glanced around with the same expression of annoyance he might direct at a mosquito.

"Whoa, young man." Nick grabbed Adam. "What do you say?"

Adam looked up at Bull, who had folded his massive arms across his chest. "'Scuse me."

Bull nodded, jowls quivering, and Adam faced Cassie.

"Are you really going to stay with us?" Before she could answer, he saw her tote bag. "Is that yours? Can I carry it? I'll show you the way to your room. It's across from ours. You'll like it. It's cool.

There are flowers on the walls and a bathroom inside."

While Cassie tried not to laugh at his excitement, he grabbed the strap of her bag and began dragging it across the marble entry.

"Easy," Nick warned. "Perhaps you'd better let Bull take that upstairs. A lady's bag can be really heavy."

He was watching Adam as if he wasn't quite sure what to do with the small boy. The flash of vulnerability tore at Cassie's heart.

"Why's it heavy?" Adam asked, giving the strap another tug before Bull lifted it from his grasp. "What's in there?"

"Rocks," Cassie replied before Nick could tell him it was impolite to ask.

Adam's eyes grew wide, as Amanda peeked around Bull's legs. Her gaze was watchful, her lips pursed.

"Okay, that's enough for now," Nick said firmly. "I have to get to work and I want to show Cassie around first, so you kids save your questions for later, okay?"

"We want to see Cassie's room, too," Adam said.

"See Cassie's room," Amanda echoed.

"You've already seen it," Nick replied.

"Let them come." Cassie hoped he wouldn't think she was usurping his authority. "They might as well get used to having me around. Before we go, I need to let Max out of the car."

"Oh, boy, you brought Max!" Adam exclaimed.

"Oh, boy," Amanda echoed.

"Who's Max?" Bull asked. "You got a kid, too?"

Cassie wondered if she'd just lost a couple of points with him.

"We didn't discuss this," Nick said stiffly as she turned away.

She knew that, but she couldn't leave Max behind to think she, too, had deserted him. Ignoring Nick's comment, Cassie hurried outside, where she could see the boxer sitting behind the steering wheel. The image made her smile. No, she hadn't discussed him with Nick; she'd been too surprised at the time by his assumption that she would stay at his place. Well, she was entitled to a surprise or two of her own.

When she released Max and snapped on his leash, he followed her obediently back to the house.

Nick was still frowning. The twins swarmed over the dog like ants on a chocolate donut and Bull turned what sounded like a chuckle into a cough before he extended a hand for the dog to sniff.

"There's fresh coffee in the kitchen," Bull told Cassie. "Let me know about breakfast."

She thanked him and he lumbered away, humming. Max had positioned himself at Cassie's side, with both Adam and Amanda stroking his short brown coat.

"See, Max likes me," Adam told Nick.

"Me, too," said Amanda, giggling when Max's pink tongue snaked out to lick her fingers.

"He won't be any trouble," Cassie said. "He's well trained and I'll make sure he doesn't get in the way." She took a deep breath, prepared to explain how the dog was grieving for Robert and why she couldn't have left the animal back home.

But Nick wasn't listening. He was staring down at Amanda, who was still giggling, with a peculiar expression on his face. Then he looked up at Cassie. The normally icy gray of his eyes had softened to smoke.

"I guess the dog can stay," he said gruffly.

Cassie wasn't about to ask why he'd given in so easily. She merely thanked him, instead.

Nick's hand hovered over Amanda's head without quite touching her, as if he wanted to but was afraid she might not like it.

"The backyard's fenced," he added. "He can have the run of it as long as he doesn't tear up the grass."

Before Cassie could thank him again, he glanced at the heavy gold Rolex on his wrist.

"Come on, kids. Let's show Cassie her room and then Daddy's got a meeting at work." The two of them were still fussing over Max. "Supervising their meals will be your responsibility. Just tell Bull what you want him to fix," Nick added.

Cassie's expression must have been skeptical, because Nick arched one eyebrow before he turned to lead the way into the house. "Appearances can be deceiving," he said over his broad shoulder. "He's a terrific cook, but don't expect him to watch the twins for you. On his list of favorites, I think kids rank right below a flat tire on his hog."

"His hog is really a motorcycle." Adam held out his fists and made revving motions, accompanied by the appropriate sound effects. "Do you think he'd give me a ride?"

"Not if he wants to live," Nick said dryly. "Maybe when you're older."

Cassie heard him mutter, "Maybe when you're thirty."

Adam might have heard him, as well. Pouting, he ducked his head.

"Is Bull's attitude toward children the reason he didn't fill in when the other nannies left?" Cassie asked quietly. The twins were rushing ahead of them up the staircase.

Nick nodded as she accompanied him across the wide entry, Max heeling at her side. "Bull has his own ideas about what his duties include. Child care isn't one of them."

Cassie would have liked to ask more about the unorthodox housekeeper. Instead, she swallowed her curiosity as Nick stopped at the foot of the staircase. The banister was carved oak, each spindle banded with brass that gleamed softly in the light from the tinted windows over the front doors. The steps were carpeted in vanilla edged with charcoal gray, the colors echoing those of the stone floor. Overhead, a massive brass chandelier hung on a heavy chain from the high ceiling.

"I'll show you to your room before I leave, and then I have to run. I've got a meeting. Last night I wrote out a rough list of things you'll need to know. Just do the best you can today and we'll deal with any questions you might have this evening when I get home."

"About what time will that be?" she asked as he indicated that she precede him up the stairs. She gestured to Max, who sank down on the tile to wait for her return.

"I wish I knew," Nick replied as he followed her. "Remember that I warned you my hours are unpredictable."

On the landing, Adam fidgeted as Amanda waited

quietly beside him. She seemed so sweet and shy; Cassie hoped that before long she'd be able to draw out the little girl.

"Occasionally, I have to travel on business," Nick continued from behind her. "In the past few weeks, I've postponed several important trips, including one to Hong Kong. Unfortunately, there are some problems I can't ignore much longer, but I'll try to stick around until you settle in."

"I appreciate that." Cassie didn't tell him she was nervous about her job. What if the twins didn't like her after all? Or wouldn't obey her? What if she found she didn't have the patience for them? Or the affinity? What if reading about children wasn't enough? She got to the top of the staircase and hesitated, even though Adam and Amanda were waiting by an open door partway down the hall. Adam was hopping on one leg.

"It's this way," Nick said as he took the lead. "Feel free to explore the rest of the house when you have time."

"Thank you." Did he expect her to make comments of her own? To ask questions? Or did someone in her position just smile and nod? Tug her forelock, stub her toe in the impossibly thick carpet and keep her gaze directed downward?

Uncertain what to do, she kept silent, although she was eager to take him up on the invitation to look through the house. What she'd already glimpsed was impressive and she wondered if he'd had a hand in it or had paid someone else. She'd learned over the years that one could tell a lot about a person from his surroundings. Either Nick was possessed of excellent taste or he'd had the good sense to hire an expert.

She knew he hadn't grown up with money; Robert had made a derogatory comment about that once. At the time she hadn't paid much attention, but now she wished she could recall what he'd said.

Whatever Nick's background might have been, he gave off the air of someone accustomed to being in charge. If she hadn't seen him around his children, she might even think him cold, but underneath his brusqueness she glimpsed an almost wistful longing she suspected he took great pains to conceal from the rest of the world.

"This is your room," Nick said, corraling Adam as the little boy attempted to dart through the doorway first. "There's a private bath, and a walk-in closet."

When Cassie went into the room, decorated in mauve and sea-foam green, Nick followed and set her tote bag on the double bed next to some papers.

"That's the list I mentioned." Expertly, he knotted his necktie, while Adam climbed onto the bed. "If you need more towels or anything, ask Bull."

Fascinated by the capable way his fingers dealt with his tie, Cassie barely managed a reply. "Nice," she finally mumbled. At least he hadn't stashed her in servants quarters in the attic.

"Do you want to see our rooms, Cassie?" Adam asked, bouncing on the mattress.

Nick frowned and she held her hand out to Adam. Did she discipline the children from the outset, or gain their trust first? Nick had given no real indication how strict or lenient he expected her to be. Fortunately, Adam let her help him off the bed. She eyed the papers on the spread. Perhaps Nick had addressed discipline on his list.

"Is there anything else you want me to know?" she asked him.

He shook his head.

To Cassie's surprise, Amanda clutched her other hand, even though she kept her face averted. Poor child was probably starved for a woman's touch in this masculine household. Pleased, Cassie allowed herself to be led from the room.

"This is it," Adam announced after pulling Cassie across the hallway.

"They each have their own room," Nick explained from directly behind her, "but so far they've preferred to stay together, and I didn't see any point in pushing the issue."

"That's probably wise," Cassie murmured over her shoulder. She'd have to take care to hide her awareness of him as a man, or he might get the wrong impression. She needed this job; what she didn't need was complications.

Up close, she could see the shadow of his whiskers. He'd put the razor in his pocket; perhaps he shaved in the car on his way to work. Did he have a lot of body hair, or was he smooth and sleek beneath his custom-tailored gray suit? He moved with the grace of an athlete, not a workaholic who spent most of his time behind a desk.

When his eyebrows rose, she realized he'd caught her staring. The direction of her thoughts horrified her. Had she learned nothing from her marriage? A flush crept up her cheeks as she felt Adam's tug on her hand and heard the puzzlement in his voice.

"Cassie? Don't you like our bedroom?"

Dazed, she glanced around. "Uh, yes, of course." It's very nice." The walls had been papered with a plaid pattern in bright red, green, blue and yellow that blurred before her gaze as she struggled to refocus her attention. The carpet was blue, the bed had a red spread and the other furniture, all scaled down for children, was painted white.

"I can see why you like this room," she added, sensing that her approval was important. "It's very colorful and you keep it nice and neat."

Shelves on two walls held a variety of games and toys. A stack of picture books sat on the floor. No doubt the children were used to an abundance of playthings, considering their father's financial situation.

She wondered what their lives had been like before they came here, and she made a mental note to ask him more about that. Surely as their nanny she needed to have some idea. Were they happy? Did they have nightmares? Behavioral problems? He'd told her very little. Amanda, especially, was timid to the point of being withdrawn. Was that normal?

Not for the first time, Cassie wondered what business she had taking on this kind of responsibility. Maybe she should have tried to get her old job at the department store back, instead, but it wouldn't have paid anything near what Nick had been desperate enough to agree to. If good intentions counted for anything, she intended to do right by the twins.

Nick was curious about what had caused the sudden blush to stain her cheeks, but he didn't have time to ask. Instead, he told the children to come back downstairs with Cassie and him; and there he showed her the utility room that housed the washer and dryer, and the kitchen, where Bull was rolling out pie dough. Max, who hadn't moved from where Cassie had left him, followed them on their tour.

With Cassie's permission, Bull offered the dog a meatball from the huge stainless-steel refrigerator. After he'd sniffed it carefully, Max swallowed the treat in one bite. Bull might not care for children, but it was easy to see he liked animals.

"Feel free to help yourself to anything you want, and to use the laundry facilities," Nick told her. "Perhaps it would be a good idea for you to take charge of the twins' clothes, too."

Bull had washed their red corduroy overalls with one of Nick's favorite white polo shirts and some of his underwear. Now the shirt and his shorts were pink.

"Give Bull a list of the groceries you need and he'll have them delivered with the regular order," he continued, trying not to notice how the creamy knit shirt Cassie was wearing hinted at her curves and played up the light tan of her arms. She didn't dress provocatively, but that trim body and platinum hair were natural signals to a man who'd been celibate for as long as he had.

When he fell silent, she merely nodded her agreement. "Of course I'll pay for Max's dog food myself," she said. "He won't be a bother."

Nick glanced at the dog, whose tongue protruded from lips pulled back into a doggie grin. His teeth were white and sharp.

"We'll work it out," Nick found himself saying. "Now I have to go." He bent to hug both children awkwardly. Adam clasped his hands around Nick's neck and gave him a wet kiss on the cheek, but Amanda merely stiffened in his embrace.

Sighing, Nick straightened, hoping he'd done the right thing in hiring Cassie. "Any questions?" he asked her.

For a moment, panic shimmered in her blue-green eyes. Then she blinked it away and thrust out her chin.

"What do they like to eat?" she asked.

"It's on the list," he replied.

"Nap times?"

"On the list."

"Days off?" she asked.

"When do you want?"

"I need Saturday afternoons and Sundays," she replied decisively.

"We'll work something out," Nick told her, ignoring his curiosity. She had a right to a break. Perhaps he could call the agency that had supplied the other nannies to him. Surely they could come up with some part-time help.

"Bedtime?" she asked. "On the list?"

He nodded, one hand on the doorknob.

"Favorite stories?" she persisted.

He started to reply that they were on the list, then hesitated. Bedtime stories were out of his league. "I have no idea," he confessed.

Her expression softened. "I'll find out and let you know."

"Okay." He tried to picture himself with the twins nestled on his lap, and failed. Instead, he imagined Cassie cuddled against him.

Suddenly, he needed to get away. Parenthood and its responsibilities were smothering him. He'd been

pleased at the idea of fatherhood in the abstract. It
had seemed a noble accomplishment. But he wasn't
equipped to deal with the reality. How could he ever
hope to measure up? "I'll see you all tonight," he
said, and fled.

By the time Nick had driven to the building that
housed his company—shaving and making several
calls on the way—and then parked his car in its usual
slot, he was himself again, confident, eager to be in
a familiar environment over which he exercised a
measure of control.

After he greeted Opal, who was seated at her sta-
tion despite the earliness of the hour, and he walked
into his spacious corner office, Nick became immediately immersed in the details of the takeover he
was conducting.

"Opal," he said over the intercom on his desk,
"send Bob and Paula in as soon as they get here.
And bring me the letters I dictated yesterday when
you're done with them, would you?"

"Of course," was her murmured reply.

For two full hours, he resisted the urge to call
home. When he did succumb, Bull answered the
phone. Nick pumped him for information about Cassie and the twins, but the ex-biker claimed ignorance.

"I ain't heard no screams," was all Bull would
say.

The second time Nick called, during a quick lunch
he ate at his desk without noticing what it was, Bull
summoned Cassie to the phone before Nick could
stop him.

"How's it going?" he asked, wondering if she'd
think he was checking up on her.

"Fine. We had lunch a little while ago—peanut-butter-and-jelly sandwiches and fruit—and I just settled them down for their naps. Did you want to talk to them?"

"Uh, no." What would he say if he did? "Don't disturb them."

"Okay. While they sleep I thought I'd unpack, run a load of their laundry and read up on art projects for children their age."

Impressed, Nick said, "Feel free to take a break yourself. I know they can be a handful, and you'll be on duty until I get home tonight, but it shouldn't be too late. One of my afternoon meetings had to be canceled."

"Should I feed them their supper, or do they wait to eat with you?" she asked.

Her query caught him off guard. Since they'd landed on his doorstep, life had been too disrupted to establish any kind of pattern. Did other parents eat with their children? He had no idea.

"Uh, if I'm not home by six you'd better feed them, I guess." The question of his eating with them hadn't come up before. The other nannies and sitters had fed them before he got home and had presented them, bathed and jammied, for good-night kisses before bustling them off to bed.

"Is there anything else?" she asked when he'd been silent for a moment.

"No, just thank you," he told her quietly.

"I'm only doing my job," she replied.

"And I appreciate it." His voice gruff, he bade her a quick goodbye and hung up before she could say anything more, feeling like a fool. Never once that afternoon, though, did he experience the knot of worry that usually twisted his gut whenever he wondered what his children were up to. And several times he found himself glancing at the clock on his office wall without his usual dread. He was actually looking forward to going home, instead of worrying that he would somehow let his children down.

As he was loading his briefcase with work, a problem erupted in Hong Kong and Nick didn't get away from the office until very late. When he let himself in the house, it was quiet and dark. Bull always went to his own apartment early to watch television, and Nick assumed Cassie and the children would be sound asleep.

Despite his fatigue, he was a little disappointed that no one was around to greet him. Sighing, he went up the stairs. When he noticed that Cassie's door was open and a light glowed from her room, some of his exhaustion slipped away.

She'd been sitting in the chaise reading, when she heard the faint sound of a door shutting downstairs. The children had been asleep for hours and Bull had disappeared, too.

Now Max raised his head and emitted a growl.

"It's okay." Cassie patted his head as she listened for footsteps on the stairs. "I'm sure it's Nick." She needed to think of him as Mr. Kincaid, she reminded herself, even though Bull called him by his first name. Bull probably didn't have trouble keeping his boss from invading his thoughts at unexpected moments as she seemed to.

Before she could discipline her mind, Nick stopped in the doorway to her room. His shoulders drooped, his hair was in disarray, the once pristine knot of his tie was unraveled and his suit jacket was draped over his arm. The light from the low, brass table lamp lit his face at an angle that highlighted his fatigue and deepened the shadows beneath his eyes.

"Sorry I'm so late," he said when she smiled and set her book aside, obviously self-conscious of her comfy old robe and fuzzy slippers. "Crisis at work. You seem to have survived your first day."

"Better than you did, from the look of you. Have you eaten? I could fix you a sandwich if you're hungry." She didn't question her urge to mother him the same way she did his children, but he waved away her offer with his hand.

"Thanks, I'm fine. What about you, though? How did it go?"

Since he appeared to be genuinely interested despite his apparent exhaustion, she hastened to reassure him.

"I think it went well." She refused to dwell on Amanda's tears when she awoke from a nightmare and wanted her mother. Cassie had managed to quiet her after a few anxious moments. No doubt there would be other rough spots, but surely she wasn't obligated to report each one to her boss. "No major crises," she added, "but I do have a few questions. Perhaps we can talk for a while tomorrow when you get home."

Since he had asked in the first place, she expected him to agree, but he surprised her by shaking his head.

"I'm afraid you'll have to manage without my input. I'm leaving for Hong Kong at the crack of dawn and I expect to be away for several days at the least."

* * *

A feeling of déjà vu settled over Nick when he came home late at night four days later with his travel kit in one hand and a garment bag slung over his shoulder. As usual, a lamp had been left burning in the entry, but beyond the pool of light the rest of the house was dark and silent.

His trip to Hong Kong had been an unqualified success, but during the long flight home he'd been edgy and impatient. Even the redheaded flight attendant who'd made a point to speak to him several times had failed to pique his interest. He hated to think it was because she hadn't been wearing an old pink robe and fuzzy slippers—an image that had popped up several times since he'd left home.

Now he mounted the stairs and suppressed a flicker of disappointment when he saw Cassie's firmly closed bedroom door. She'd probably turned in hours ago, and he had no business speculating about what she wore beneath that robe. Instead, he should be worrying that her dog might hear him and raise the alarm. But the silence was unbroken.

He eased open the door to Adam's bedroom, where the little boy and his sister still slept together. A night-light shaped like a clown face glowed softly, illuminating the sleeping forms in Adam's bed.

A bubble of affection rose in Nick's throat as he permitted himself to lean over and kiss his son's forehead. At times like these his reservations about parenthood faded; these children were his flesh and blood. His love for them was unquestionable.

Adam stirred and murmured something in his sleep, but he didn't waken. After gazing down at him for a moment, Nick brushed the hair from Amanda's cheek and kissed her, as well. She smelled like soap and he felt a sudden urge to fill his lungs with the homey scent.

Adam stirred again, touching Amanda with his arm. She frowned in her sleep and Nick straightened, not wanting to frighten either of them if they should awaken. As he did, he noticed the glow of a light from beyond the partially closed door to Amanda's empty room. Puzzled, Nick tiptoed over and pushed the door open. When he saw the strange old woman sitting in the rocking chair, reading, he nearly yelped.

"What are you doing here?" he demanded in a harsh whisper.

With her white hair, wire-framed glasses, quilted robe and felt slippers, the woman sitting in the rocking chair reminded him of Santa's wife. Looking up, she smiled at Nick and pressed one finger to her lips. Then she rose and led the way out into the hall, beckoning for him to follow.

Shutting the door behind them, he asked, "Who the hell are you? Where's Cassie?" He glanced at the tightly closed door to her bedroom. Had she quit already? What was going on? He'd been so eager to complete his business in Hong Kong and get home that he hadn't bothered to call the past couple of days. Now he wished he had.

"I'm Mrs. Beagle," whispered the old lady, extending a thin, heavily veined hand. On one of her bony fingers was a large ring encrusted with diamonds. "You must be Mr. Kincaid, father to those precious angels."

Gingerly, he shook her hand, careful not to crush the fragile bones beneath his impatient grip as she looked him up and down with a smile of open approval.

"Mrs. Wainright described you to a tee."

That roused his curiosity. Just what had Cassie said about him?

"Where is she?" he repeated.

"Gone," Mrs. Beagle replied.

The remark sent his stomach into a downward spiral.

"For the weekend."

Vaguely, Nick remembered promising her Saturday afternoons and Sundays off. He'd meant to make arrangements before he left, but he'd forgotten.

"Are you from the agency?" he asked.

"Oh, no, dear, I'm from the senior citizens' center."

He narrowed his eyes. "Do you have any references?"

Her grin was impish despite her age. "Only six children and fourteen grandchildren," she replied. "I live with my son, Charles, and his wife, over by the church on Maple. He's a dentist. Mrs. Wainright saw my ad on the center's bulletin board and hired me to fill in on weekends."

"Indeed," Nick drawled.

"Yes, she told me she needed Saturday afternoons off to visit someone. We decided I'd stay over and watch the children until she comes back on Sunday evenings. It gives my son and his wife a bit of privacy on the weekends." Her eyes twinkled.

Nick was still wondering whom Cassie needed so badly to visit on Saturdays. To his surprise, annoyance churned in his stomach. Couldn't she have stuck around until he'd returned to deal with all this? Apparently not.

Mrs. Beagle clearly expected him to make some comment.

"So," Nick asked her, resigned to waiting until Cassie came back to straighten out the situation, "what am I paying you?"

"Nothing, dear," she replied. "Mrs. Wainright promised to take care of that herself, out of her wages. It must be someone very special she goes to see, don't you think?"

Nick frowned. Clearly, there was someone in Cassie's life who meant a great deal to her—enough that she was willing to leave her charges with a stranger and jeopardize the best paying nanny's job on the entire east side of Lake Washington. He could hardly wait to find out who the mystery person was.

Chapter Four

Later that same night, Cassie stood at the window of her bedroom and stared out at the moon, hanging like a silver Christmas ornament against the dark sky. Sleep eluded her as she thought about the visit she'd had with her mother that afternoon.

"I'll see you next week," Cassie told her mother, bending to kiss the dry cheek.

As Cassie straightened, Adele Hansen had darted a glance at her. The older woman's forehead was puckered into a frown, but she remained silent as her gaze went back to the scene through the window of her room at Woodlake.

Cassie sighed, heart aching. Sometimes her mother remembered who she was and they were able to talk a little. Today wasn't one of those times.

As she did every Saturday afternoon, Cassie had asked about the food, commented on the ducks that swam in the pond outside the window, checked Mom's supply of tissues and the batteries for her portable radio. Except for an occasional unrelated comment or agitated question, her mother sat quietly, hands folded, and stared out the window, her mind a hostage to encroaching memory loss and confusion.

Cassie longed to reassure her that the overdue nursing home bill was finally paid and to promise she would do her best to guarantee her mother's life remained as calm as possible. Cassie would have liked to describe the twins and Bull and, most of all, her new boss. She wanted to confide her anger and hurt over Robert's betrayal, still fresh despite his death, her fear that her financial security might be taken away and her loss of faith in her own judgment.

Robert's infidelity had shaken her to the core. She knew they'd had problems, but she had never thought he would cheat on her. Now she felt like a naive fool.

Cassie wished her mother were able to promise that time would heal her pain, that someday she'd find the man of her dreams. But she realized that what her mother would have said, if she were able, was for Cassie to take charge of her life and not wait for someone else to rescue her.

She had wanted to say that she was trying. Never sure how much her mother actually heard or what might upset her, Cassie kept her comments to herself. Instead, she pressed a hand to her mother's bony shoulder and whispered, "I love you."

For a moment something had flickered in the faded eyes. Cassie's breath caught. Sometimes the curtains of confusion parted for a fleeting instant, to be replaced by a gleam of recognition, even a relevant question.

"Where's my breakfast?" Adele had demanded instead in a querulous voice, although it was now the middle of the afternoon. "You forgot to bring my breakfast and you're out of uniform again. I'm going to speak to your supervisor about your carelessness."

"I'll see about it right away," Cassie had replied, swallowing her disappointment. "I'm sorry for the oversight." Taking her purse, she left the room and headed for the main desk.

"Has my mother been eating her meals today?" she'd asked the attendant seated at the computer.

The woman knew Cassie. She keyed in an entry and studied the computer screen. "Adele ate most of her breakfast and half of her sandwich at lunch." Her smile had been edged with compassion. "Did she know you today?"

Cassie had been forced to swallow the sudden lump in her throat. "Not this time. Thank you, Mary."

"Maybe next week."

Cassie dug her keys from her purse.

"Perhaps. I'll see you then." By the time she'd crossed the lawn to her car, she'd grown calm again. Sliding behind the wheel of the white Porshe Robert had bought her for their second anniversary, she started the engine.

Too bad she couldn't have gone straight back to work. She'd had a feeling that being with the twins would help take her mind off the past half hour.

Instead other duties had called. She had dropped Max off at home earlier and she'd needed to check in with Emma, look through the mail and see if Walter had left a message.

She'd thought about calling and making sure Mrs. Beagle was coping. Other than that, there had been nothing more Cassie could do until the next evening.

Now Max snored peacefully as Cassie stared out her bedroom window and wondered what the time difference was in Hong Kong and whether her employer was asleep or clinching deals of international significance.

The thought of Nick, his face shadowed with fatigue and the stubble of a beard as she'd last seen him, made her uncomfortable. Self-consciously, she folded her arms across her breasts, covered only by the sheer white cotton of her nightie.

After her visit at Woodlake, she'd had supper with Emma, relating a few of the things she'd wanted to tell her mother today: how cute Adam looked walking Max on his leash, the shy hug Amanda had given Cassie after she'd taught the child to tie her shoes, Bull's tricks of putting orange extract in the French toast and cinnamon in hot chocolate.

Subjects like that were safer than what was really on Cassie's mind. Emma would only worry and there was nothing she could do to help.

Now Cassie rubbed her hands along her bare arms. Despite the mildness of the night air, her skin felt chilled.

Had she been too hasty in hiring Mrs. Beagle without consulting Nick first? Would he appreciate her initiative or resent her presumption?

She'd had no choice, she told herself as she moved from her post at the window and climbed back into the big bed. It was bad enough that he'd left for Hong Kong without taking care of the matter himself. She'd been on her own all week, with very little help from Mr. Wylie.

Oh, Nick had called to check in and she'd actually talked to him a couple of times—if answering his rapid-fire questions could be classified as a conversation. His concern was for his children's welfare, not for their new nanny's jitters or her personal obligations. As soon as he heard that Adam and Amanda seemed to be adjusting to her presence with a minimum of fuss, he'd hurriedly ended the conversation before she could ask any questions of her own. Before she could suggest he speak to his children himself.

Neither had they asked about his return, she realized now. If was as if they were used to people disappearing from their lives. Cassie felt a twinge of guilt. Had they believed her when she'd promised to return Sunday afternoon?

It was too late to worry about that now. And she'd have time enough to explain Mrs. Beagle to Nick when he got back on Monday. Meanwhile, she needed sleep.

Perhaps she'd go back to Nick's early tomorrow and put the twins to bed herself. That way she could reassure them that they hadn't been abandoned yet again. Maybe she'd tell them about visiting her mother, at least the part they might understand. If they knew where she went when she left them, it might help.

Cassie visited her mother every Saturday afternoon without fail. In her present condition, Adele wouldn't notice if Cassie missed a week, but *she* would know.

Cassie switched off the bedside lamp and thumped her pillow. For now there wasn't anything she could do but hope that the IRS found nothing in their investigation and that Miles could keep the company afloat until they were done. Frustrating as it was, all Cassie could do was wait.

When she drove up Nick's driveway the next evening, the first thing Cassie noticed was his shiny black Mercedes parked in front of the house. Her stomach sinking in dismay, she got out of her own car and freed Max from the back seat, as Adam burst through the double front doors.

"Hi, Cassie," he hollered.

He ran ahead of Amanda and threw his arms around Max, who had rushed joyously to meet him. Cassie returned his greeting distractedly as her gaze collided with Nick's.

He was standing in the doorway, thumbs hooked into the wide leather belt he wore with faded jeans and a knit shirt that hugged his broad shoulders. The outfit confirmed what his more formal clothing had only hinted at: he was in excellent condition.

Adam let Max go and hugged Cassie's legs, trapping her as Amanda extended a hand to Max, who licked it exuberantly.

"He missed me," she said shyly.

"Of course he did. I missed you, too." Painfully aware that Nick was still watching her from the porch, Cassie leaned down to kiss Adam's cheek.

Where was Mrs. Beagle? Had Nick dismissed her? Would he fire Cassie in front of the children? As she grabbed her tote bag and followed the twins to the house, her feet felt as though her shoes were made from cement.

"Daddy brought us presents, T-shirts from the airport. He brought something for you, too, but he wouldn't tell us what it is," Adam volunteered as he skipped along in front of her.

"That was so you wouldn't spill the beans," Nick drawled. Worn western boots added to his height.

"What beans?" Adam asked. "Did you bring Cassie beans?"

"That's just an expression," she told him. She nearly got a crick in her neck, looking up at Nick on the porch. "How nice of you to think of me," she said politely as she searched his expression for possible clues to his mood. No doubt his poker face stood him in good stead with his business rivals, but she found it annoying to the extreme. If he was going to fire her, let him get it over with.

"Amanda," she said with a touch of defiance, "how did you like Mrs. Beagle?"

Amanda kept stroking Max's wrinkled forehead as he crowded closer, tail wagging. "She's nice. She played Chutes and Ladders with us and then she read us stories."

"We baked gingerbread men before she left," Adam added, scratching the dog's ear and earning himself a soggy swipe of Max's tongue.

Cassie's gaze collided with Nick's over his daughter's head. "Left?" she echoed.

"I sent her home a little while ago." Nick's mouth bore a smile that didn't reach his eyes.

"How was your trip?" Cassie asked quickly.

"Productive." His eyebrows rose mockingly. "How was your time off?"

"Relaxing." She glanced at the twins, but they appeared to be totally focused on the dog.

"I'm sorry that I took matters into my own hands and hired Mrs. Beagle," she began, and then she bit her lip. There was no reason to sound so apologetic. "I did tell you that I needed Saturday afternoons free."

Why? Nick wondered. Who was so important to her that she couldn't go one weekend without seeing that person? A lover? Had she and her husband the kind of open marriage other people Nick knew indulged in? He was curious about what she'd say if he admitted he'd thought of her nearly as much as he had his own children. No doubt those turquoise eyes of hers would widen in surprise, as if she had no idea what he was talking about. Nor would she admit she'd thought of him once or twice—even if she had.

He was also curious about whom she'd want as a lover—an older man who oozed success from his pores or a sweaty young stud? As soon as Nick realized the direction of his thoughts, he snapped them back to the present.

"That's right, you did mention it. I meant to take care of the matter before I left." He refused to give in to his curiosity and ask where she'd been. "I wrapped things up early, so I decided to come home," he added as he followed her through the door. "How was your weekend?" The question slipped out before he could stop himself.

"I've only been gone since yesterday."

She sounded defensive, but he thought he heard a thread of sadness in her voice, too. Was she involved in a relationship that wasn't going well? Perhaps because of the threat to her finances. Men weren't the only ones who attracted gold diggers.

Nick raised his eyebrows at her reply. "Let me rephrase that. How was your day off?" As soon as the words were out, he regretted his sarcasm, but Cassie had the grace to look uncomfortable.

"It was fine."

It was Nick's turn to feel hot color run up his cheeks. She was right; she had *told* him she needed some free time. Had he expected her to work seven days a week?

When the business deal in Hong Kong had begun falling apart, he'd shoved everything else aside—including responsibility for his children—and hopped on a plane.

He could feel the ghosts hovering around him. He was the product of an indifferent father—hell, of no father, if one wanted to be accurate—and now he was inheriting the legacy. It was preordained: he didn't have it in him to be a good parent.

Raking a hand through his hair, Nick jerked away. It wasn't the twins' fault they'd been saddled with a poor excuse for a mother and a father who had failure programmed into his genes.

"I'm sorry," he growled. "I forgot about your time off."

Instantly Cassie brightened, but her smile contained not a hint of triumph. "That's okay. I'm sure you had a lot on your mind."

"Mrs. Beagle seems very competent," he added grudgingly. "We had quite a talk."

Cassie chewed her lip for a moment. "I admit I didn't go through an agency," she blurted, "but Mrs. Beagle is well-known at the local seniors' center, and

I did check out her references. You might know them—the Pattersons down the road from you and the Ingrams next door to them. She's watched their children and they gave her glowing reviews.''

"I know the Ingrams," Nick admitted. "Chuck used to be the Seahawks' attorney. He got me tickets for a couple of football games."

"His wife sounded nice on the phone, and she said they have a new baby."

Nick hadn't known that. He'd met Naomi only once, but he remembered that Chuck had three older children by his first marriage. "You're certainly thorough," he told Cassie. "Maybe I should have hired you as the personnel manager for my company. It sounds as if your talents are wasted here."

"I thought the twins might like an older person," Cassie said, relieved that Nick seemed to accept what she'd done. "Like a grandmother." Cassie realized she had no idea if they had real grandparents or not. "Another grandmother," she amended hastily. "I mean, in case they have one already, or even two." She grimaced, aware that she was babbling.

Nick made no move to help her out. A grin played at the corners of his mouth.

"Do they have grandparents?" she was finally forced to ask.

"More or less. Janine's parents live in Florida. I've met them only a couple of times and their priorities don't seem to include grandchildren. My mother has a condo in San Francisco. She comes up fairly often, but she's just had a hip replaced." His frown deepened.

Cassie waited, but no more information seemed to

be forthcoming. She sought to change the subject before the silence became awkward.

"When did you get back from your trip?"

Briefly, Nick described walking in on Mrs. Beagle the night before. Cassie gasped when he admitted he'd thought for a few moments that she'd quit.

"I didn't realize," she murmured apologetically. "If there had been another way…"

He shrugged.

At least he didn't point out that she could have just stayed until he returned. Cassie thought about that. Funny that he hadn't asked what business had been so pressing that she couldn't wait. Why didn't she just tell him? It wasn't as if she was ashamed of her mother's illness.

"No need for you to pay Mrs. Beagle," he said. "I'll take care of her wages myself."

"Why did she tell you that?"

"Because I asked her," he replied.

Before Cassie could think of an appropriate comment, he stuck his head back outside and called to Amanda and Adam, who were romping with Max across the velvety green front lawn.

"Can we take him up to our room?" Adam asked when they ascended the steps.

Nick glanced at Cassie.

"It's okay with me," she said.

Nick gave his permission. Kids plus dog thundered past.

"Careful on the stairs," Cassie warned.

"Like trying to stop the tide," Nick muttered as he followed her inside, admiring the way her tailored gray slacks hugged her trim hips. With them she wore a short-sleeved lavender sweater and muted purple suede sandals. She was only of average height, but her legs in the tapered pants seemed to go on forever.

He had to remind himself that his luck with women was lousy. After his marriage to Janine, a serious relationship no longer interested him and he knew better than to get involved with an employee, even one as appealing as Cassie.

He was vaguely aware that she was looking at him and he wondered what she was thinking. The soft pastel of her sweater intensified the blue of her eyes below her thin, arching brows. His attention wandered to her mouth. As if she could tell the direction of his thoughts, she pressed her lips together.

He ran a hand over his face. It must be delayed jet lag, he reasoned, that had him staring at her like a sex-starved fool. Why else was he acting so out of character?

Pulling a small package out of his pocket, he thrust it at her. "It's not much," he found himself saying as she took it from him.

"I didn't expect anything."

While she unwrapped it cautiously, he pictured the aquamarine earrings he'd seen in the airport shop. They matched the ring on her finger and reminded him of the unusual blue of her eyes, but he'd known they would only make her uncomfortable. He'd settled on a small jade pendant, instead.

"Oh," she exclaimed softly, holding up the pendant. "It's lovely."

Nick glanced at the tiny shamrock hanging from a thin gold chain. "For luck," he said gruffly. He would have liked to fasten it around her neck, but he resisted.

"Thank you." The silence stretched awkwardly between them. "Is there anything else you wanted to discuss?" she asked. "If not, I should probably spend a little time with the children before I put them to bed. Unless you were going to? You must have missed them a lot."

Ignoring the question in her voice, he thought of the work that waited for him in his briefcase. "You go ahead."

If she disapproved of his attitude, he couldn't see it in her expression. Before either of them could add anything, Adam poked his head over the banister.

"Cassie, come look at our Hong Kong shirts," he shouted.

She waved back at him. "I'll be right there, sweetie."

Nick watched his head disappear again. "Do you think they're happy?" he asked Cassie.

"Happy?" she gave him a searching glance. "Of course. Why do you ask?"

He shrugged. "No reason." He remembered how scared they'd been when he picked them up at the airport, clinging together for support as an airline attendant hovered anxiously, and he knew a sudden urge to make sure they were better off with him than they'd been with their mother.

If only he had some clue how to go about it. He hadn't even thought about bringing them presents until he'd noticed the earrings on display at an airport shop. It was only after he bought the pendant that he realized he needed something for them, as well. Even then, he'd had to guess at their sizes. Was that something a father should know?

"Thank you again for the pendant."

Cassie headed up the staircase, while Nick forced himself to walk away instead of gaping after her like some hormone-crazed teenaged boy. Perhaps keeping his thoughts—and his hands—off the help was going to be tougher than he'd originally expected.

The next morning was a disaster.

"I don't think they should be eating that sugary cereal," Nick announced, walking through the breakfast room with a cup of coffee during breakfast. "I'd rather you gave them oatmeal."

"Oatmeal, yuck!" Adam exclaimed with his mouth full of rainbow loops. "I don't like oatmeal."

"Yuck," Amanda echoed. "Don't like oatmeal."

"Young man, don't talk with your mouth full," Nick told his son in an intimidating tone.

Adam's lower lip stuck out, while Amanda's eyes flooded with tears. Cassie half rose from her chair, intending an offstage protest, but she was too late.

Adam's glass tipped over, sending a wave of orange juice across the table. With a horrified expression, he watched the juice spread as Cassie began mopping it up with a kitchen towel.

"I'm sorry," Adam mumbled. "It was a accident."

"I know, sweetie. Finish your breakfast."

"I'm not hungry." Next to him, Amanda began to cry.

Cassie glanced at Nick.

"What did I do?" he asked defensively as Bull poked his head around the corner to see what the noise was all about.

Nick glared and Bull glared back. Finally the housekeeper glanced at Cassie, muttered something and disappeared. Nick made an exasperated gesture with his free hand and retreated.

"Try to eat a little," Cassie told Adam. "How about a slice of kiwi? That comes from the place where koala bears live. Remember we looked at their picture in that book with the kangaroos in it?"

"I remember." Adam poked at the green fruit with his fork. "What are the black things?"

"Edible seeds."

He looked doubtful, then he smiled. "Okay."

Cassie was congratulating herself for a crisis diverted, when the little boy continued.

"Daddy's mad. Now he'll send us away on a big airplane."

"Mommy doesn't want us," Amanda added. "We'll have to go to an orphanage."

"Uncle Cosmos said he wasn't raising another man's brats," Adam volunteered.

Cassie's heart ached for them. Could their mother have actually threatened to send them to an orphanage? Or chosen a new boyfriend over her own children? Feeling ill, Cassie squatted between them. "I'm sure your mommy would never really do that." She tried to put conviction in her voice. "And your daddy wouldn't have hired me if he was planning to send you away, would he?"

Adam brightened visibly and even Amanda looked relieved. Impulsively, Cassie gave each child a quick hug. "You can have rainbow loops every morning if you want," she vowed rashly. "I'll square things with your dad."

From the hallway, Nick tried to control the frustration and guilt that had ripped at him on hearing his children's confessions. He'd suspected when Janine took off with them that he should have tried harder to get them back. He'd known nothing about caring for babies, so small and helpless, and he remembered how terrified he'd been of making a mistake that would harm them. Had he been secretly relieved that she'd taken them off his hands? What kind of a father was he, to let them go without a fight?

He'd taken the easy way out and his children were paying the price. He might like to shake Janine until her diamond studs fell out, but she wasn't the only one to blame. The twins were his own flesh and blood, and he'd let them down.

Filled with self-disgust, Nick grabbed his briefcase and headed out the door before he overheard any more painful revelations.

"Hey, man, get your head in the game!" Bill Radich darted around Nick, twisted away from his futile attempt at blocking and sent the basketball swishing through the net.

"Like shooting fish in a barrel," he taunted as Nick dove after the ball.

Nick bared his teeth and drove past Bill. The shot went wide, hitting the backboard before it bounced harmlessly off the rim. Leaping high, Bill snagged the rebound and scored.

"You still play like a girl," he jeered.

Nick had to grin at the ancient insult, devised when they'd grown up on the same street. Now Bill was the head mechanic for a local car dealer, but they got together whenever their schedules permitted for a furious game of one-on-one. Nick still preferred it to racquetball or tennis.

"A girl's all you could beat," he replied, dribbling slowly as he looked for an opening.

"How're the kids?" Bill asked, just as Nick broke with the ball. He hesitated and Bill stole it from under his hand.

"Child's play," Bill gasped after he'd sunk the winning basket.

"You distracted me." Nick grabbed a towel and mopped off his face, while Bill stood with his head lowered, catching his breath.

"Whatever works."

Bill picked up the ball and his own towel, looping it around his neck while Nick headed for the showers. Bill and his wife had daughters, both in grade school, and a baby on the way. Fatherhood appeared to rest easily on his shoulders. But he hadn't grown up in a one-parent household. His mom and dad still lived in the same house and they baby-sat often. Six months earlier, Bill had bought an older house two blocks away from them. Nick wondered if Bill had any idea how lucky he was.

"So how's it going?" Bill asked when they stopped at their lockers. "Having the kids living with you cramp your style any?"

Nick grinned without answering. Since Janine had left, Bill persisted in assuming he led the life of a swinging bachelor. Nick hated to disillusion him.

"I hired a nanny," Nick said as he stripped off his damp T-shirt.

"What's she like?" Bill asked. "Knowing you, she's got blond hair and a Scandinavian accent."

He wore an envious expression Nick knew was mostly sham. Bill hadn't looked at another woman since the day he met Sharon. His marriage was one of the few Nick would call successful.

"Well, she's blond," Nick replied, tossing aside the rest of his clothes and heading for the shower. He pictured Cassie in the jeans and blouse she usually wore at work, her hair pulled back and her expression relaxed as she read to the twins.

"Pretty?" Bill asked.

Nick found himself reluctant to answer. "I guess. Yeah. Silver-blond hair, blue-green eyes, body from the cover of *Sports Illustrated,* swimsuit issue."

Bill groaned. "I guess," he echoed. "Getting anywhere with her?" he asked, catching up with Nick.

Nick raised his eyebrows as he turned on the water and stepped beneath its icy spray. "Who said I was trying?"

Bill just laughed as Nick turned his back. "Like I don't know you, man."

"I did make her sign a six-month contract," Nick found himself volunteering.

"Where'd you locate her?" Bill asked as Nick ducked his head beneath the spray. "Agency?"

Nick came up sputtering and sluiced the water from his face with one hand. Briefly, he explained about Cassie as he toweled off. "The kids seem to like her," he concluded, putting on fresh clothes. "Got time for a beer?" Maybe he'd ask for a few pointers with the kids.

Bill glanced at the wall clock. "Nah. Sharon has a doctor's appointment and I want to go with her."

Nick was partly relieved. What could Bill have said if he confessed that he didn't know how to be a real father to his own children? Would Bill have

looked at him with horror? With pity? Better Nick
kept his feelings of inadequacy to himself.

"Maybe next time," he said.

"You bet." Bill shook the hand Nick offered and
clapped him on the back. "I'm parked on the other
side, so I'll see you later. Meanwhile, take it easy on
that nanny. What's her name, anyway?"

"Cassie," Nick replied. "Her name's Cassie." He
was annoyed to notice that the tension that had
drained away on the basketball court was back, tightening his stomach like a vise.

"So," Bill asked, trailing Nick through the door,
"when do we get to meet this paragon?"

"Never!" Nick exclaimed. "I haven't forgotten
how hard your wife tried to fix me up after my divorce was final. All I need is for her to get ideas
about Cassie." Nick himself already had more ideas
about her than he needed.

Chapter Five

"Do it again!" Adam cried.

Bull flipped another flapjack into the air. Both Adam and Amanda applauded enthusiastically, while he tried not to look pleased.

"Eat your breakfast before it gets cold," Cassie told them, leaning her hip against the counter as she sipped her coffee.

"You'd think they'd get tired of pancakes," Bull grumbled, stacking them on a plate.

"Not as long as you keep making animal shapes," Cassie replied, taking the full plate to the table and serving Adam and Amanda before she went back to refill her coffee cup.

Bull stirred more batter and began pouring it onto the griddle.

"I was a cook in the army," he said with a gap-toothed grin. "Drove the brass crazy when their flap-jacks weren't regulation shape."

"I'll bet." Cassie tried to picture him in a uniform, and failed. She watched a goldfish and then a turtle take shape on the griddle.

"I want a doggie like Max," Adam called out.

Bull glared over his massive shoulder. "I ain't in the army anymore."

"What's that mean?" Adam asked.

"It means I don't follow no orders from no midget."

"Please may I?" Adam amended.

Bull sighed. "I'll see what I can do."

"First you eat what you already have on your plate," Cassie told Adam. She glanced at Amanda. "How are you doing?"

"Fine." The little girl took another bite of bacon. "Can I have a bunny?"

Bull nodded, grumbling. Cassie began to suspect his dislike of children was all an act.

In the doorway, Max waited patiently for a hand-out. Bull made no secret of his fondness for animals. He slipped Max a treat whenever the dog was in the kitchen, while Cassie pretended not to notice.

"How did you and Mr. Kincaid meet?" she asked. Ever since Bull had first opened the front door to her, she'd wondered how his path had crossed Nick's. The two men were as different as moonshine and blended Scotch.

"We were college roommates."

Cassie's mouth dropped open. "Really?" she squeaked.

"Whatsamatter? Dint ya think I went to college?"

he demanded, his small eyes narrowed below the wild thatch of his eyebrows.

Heat raced across Cassie's cheeks. She hadn't meant to offend him. "Of course not," she blustered. "You two just seem so different. I wouldn't have thought you'd have a lot of, um, shared interests, that's all." Oh, great, now she'd offended him, just when she'd thought he was warming up to her a little.

Bull's glare deepened and then he slapped the spatula against his thigh. Laughter rolled up from his chest and boomed across the kitchen as his jowls quivered. "Gotcha."

Cassie blinked, confused. "I beg your pardon?"

"I didn't go to no college," Bull told her.

With a shrug, he scooped up the pancakes and took them to the children, who pounced like hungry bears on a honeycomb. Cassie watched to make sure they didn't need her help.

"Want any more?" Bull asked her.

"No, thanks." She'd already had several.

When he came back to the stove, she eyed him warily. "I didn't mean to offend you."

"Aw, shucks," he replied, "none taken. I was only pullin' your leg. Truth is, I never finished high school. All I cared about was motorcycles. But I got in with a bad crowd. Before I knew it, I had a police record. Nothin' big, though. Just petty stuff." He hesitated as he wiped drips of pancake batter off the counter.

The twins seemed preoccupied with their breakfast, so Cassie waited silently for him to continue.

"Me and the boss met when I tried to bash his head in," Bull said.

This time she was ready. "Oh, sure. He was so impressed that he hired you on the spot."

Bull wiped his hands on the dish towel tucked into his ample waist and poured himself a cup of coffee. "I don't know about that." Above the rim of his cup, his eyes danced and the silver ring piercing his eyebrow wobbled. "You don't believe me."

"'Fool me once...'" Cassie recited with a smile.

"It's true," he insisted, slurping his coffee and then wiping his mouth with the back of his hand. "A guy hired me to rough Nick up, to sort of discourage him from bidding against the guy on a certain piece of property."

Again Cassie glanced at the children, who were carrying on an animated conversation of their own.

"You're kidding, right?" she asked Bull. "You weren't really going to beat up Nick."

Bull shrugged, draining the rest of his coffee before he answered. "Nah, I was going to pound his head in with a tire iron. That's what the other guy paid me for. You see, I was trying to break into the enforcement business and he was my first serious customer."

Bull's story sounded like a low-budget movie. "You beat people up for money?"

"Not anymore. I told you I didn't have no college degree," Bull explained. "A man's gotta eat."

"So how did you go from rookie enforcer to male housekeeper?" she asked skeptically.

"Basically, Nick offered me a better deal." Bull's cheeks turned a dusky red and he scratched his stomach absently. "'Course, that was after he beat the tar out of me and convinced me I was in the wrong line of work."

A sudden knot formed in Cassie's stomach at the image of Nick being threatened by a thug with a tire iron. Bull was immense; Nick could have been badly hurt.

"He won the fight and then he offered you a job?"

Bull nodded. "Yeah. First he asked who sent me. Of course I wouldn't tell him, so he threatened to smash my kneecaps with my own weapon. That's when I decided it was time for a career change."

Cassie swallowed convulsively and took a quick sip of coffee. "Oh, my." Either Bull was a very creative storyteller or his was the oddest job interview in history. "I suppose you kept still and refused to rat on your boss?" she asked.

It was Bull's turn to glance at the kids.

"Hell, no. I sang like a canary. Then I said something about wishing I had my old job back, as an army cook. One thing led to another and I been here for over two years." His expansive gesture took in the entire gourmet kitchen.

"So you knew the twins' mother?" Cassie asked. She was curious what kind of woman could have given up her own children—and could have left Nick.

Bull shook his head. "Nah. She was long gone when I showed up. Nick lived here alone, had a cleaning woman come in twice a week and did his own cooking."

The strength of Cassie's disappointment caught her by surprise. Not only was she curious for the children's sake, she wondered what kind of woman Nick would have cared about enough to make his wife.

As Cassie rinsed out her mug and put it into the

dishwasher, she realized Bull was still watching her. "That's quite a story," she said primly.

"You like Nick?" he asked.

His question surprised her. Instantly, she became cautious. "I don't know him very well, but he seems like a reasonable employer."

Bull looked disgusted. "You got a boyfriend?"

She shook her head. "I'm a widow. My husband was killed in a car accident a few weeks ago."

"Yeah, I knew that. He was with some other broad, right? So you ain't exactly crying over his sudden elimination, are you?"

Her eyes widened at Bull's perception. "No, I've been mad as hell at him," she admitted.

"Cassie, we're done," Adam called as he got down from the table.

As soon as she'd wiped both his and his sister's sticky hands and faces, she settled them in front of the family room TV and went back to the kitchen to clean up from breakfast. Bull tried to run her off, but she insisted on taking care of the dishes and mopping up the dribbles of syrup on the table and the floor.

"You think Nick's a handsome guy?" he asked abruptly as she was putting the butter dish back into the refrigerator.

His expression was so patently innocent that Cassie's instincts went on red alert. "Oh, no, you don't." She shook a warning finger under his broad nose. "Don't even think about it."

"About what?"

He became engrossed in buffing imaginary fingerprints from a leaded glass cupboard door. Subtle he wasn't.

"My relationship with Mr. Kincaid is strictly professional, nothing more," Cassie said firmly.

Now Bull looked up, a smug grin on his round face. "Yeah, I understand. But I see how he watches you."

Cassie's face flamed. He did? Worse yet, had Bull noticed *her* watching *Nick?*

"I meant what I said." She tried to inject more forcefulness into her tone. "He's divorced, I'm widowed and we have nothing in common."

Bull gave her a jaunty thumbs up. "You're right," he said. "I gotcha."

For a couple of days Cassie was on her guard, watching for any indication that Bull had some crazy matchmaking scheme in mind. Finally, when she was convinced she'd either misinterpreted his comments or succeeded in disabusing him of any notions in that direction, she began to relax.

She and the children had established a loose routine. In the morning after breakfast they usually went on an outing, then returned home for lunch and a nap, during which Cassie read all the library books on child care she could get her hands on. In the afternoon there was playtime, with a little basic education thrown in or art projects Bull reluctantly allowed them to display on the refrigerator. Then came dinner, baths, story time and bed.

Nick usually got home from work after the twins were asleep. If he looked in on them, he did it when Cassie wasn't around. He brought a briefcase full of work with him and disappeared into his office as soon as he'd finished the meal Bull served before retiring to his own apartment.

One evening Cassie was on her way to the kitchen for a cup of tea. It had been a long day and a mild headache tapped at her temples.

When she walked past the dining room, she saw Nick seated at the handsome cherry table. His briefcase was open and papers were spread in a circle around his dinner dishes.

He raised his head from what he'd been reading. "Hello, Cassie. How was your day?"

Pausing in the arched doorway, she returned his greeting. The sight of him eating alone contradicted the image of the successful single man who went out every night with a different woman. As far as she knew, he hadn't been on a date since she'd started working there a couple of weeks before.

"Don't you ever relax?" she asked.

"I am relaxed."

"You're still working."

Nick glanced down at the papers as if he'd forgotten their existence. His expression was rueful.

"I'm closing a complicated deal next week and there aren't enough hours at the office to go over everything I need to know."

He held a pen in one hand and a half-full wineglass in the other. The top two buttons of his shirt were undone; his dark hair was in disarray and whiskers shadowed his lean cheeks.

Cassie felt a surge of tenderness and her fingers itched to smooth the hair off his forehead. Her instinct was maternal, she told herself, a carryover from mothering the twins all day.

"Well, I'll leave you to it," she murmured.

"Have you had dinner?" he asked.

"I ate with the children."

"Would you like a glass of wine?"

She shook her head. "No, thanks. I was going to make myself a cup of tea."

"You could bring it back here and keep me company." Nick sounded almost wistful, a smile hovering at the corners of his mouth. Did he ever get lonely?

Cassie realized that she had no idea whether he had friends, other interests, a special woman he was seeing. Had his life been turned upside down by the arrival of his children? Even if that was so, now that she was here he was free to resume whatever mad social whirl he'd been part of, if he wished.

"Okay," she replied, ignoring the little shiver of warning that sizzled through her. "I'll just be a minute." Except for the faint sound of Bull's television, the house was silent. Even Max was asleep in the upstairs hallway.

Moments later, she was back with her tea.

"There's fresh coffee in the kitchen and Bull made a key lime pie today," she said as she set down her cup. "Can I get you something?"

Nick rubbed a hand across his forehead and then he pushed back his chair. "You don't need to wait on me. Would you like a piece of pie?" His smile deepened the lines etched into the sides of his face.

"You look tired. Stay where you are," she told him, reaching for his plate. "Are you done with your dinner?"

He sank back down. "Yes, thanks. I don't expect you to clean up after me. With two active toddlers, I'm sure you do that enough."

His hand rested on the table. The sight of it sent a warm feeling spreading through her.

"You must be tired, too. Do the kids wear you out?"

"Don't worry about me. You certainly pay me enough for a few extra duties," she said without thinking.

Instantly, his smile vanished. "Don't feel you have to entertain me," he said stiffly. "After they're in bed, your time's your own."

She bit her lip. Had she sounded as though she considered him one of her extra duties? "I know that. If you don't mind, I'd enjoy having dessert with you."

His shoulders relaxed visibly and his grin returned, softening the harshness of his mouth.

"Cut me a big slice, would you, and one for yourself. You don't look as if you have to count calories."

He'd stacked his dinner dishes neatly, so she took them when she went. In moments, she was back with the pie, his coffee, sugar and cream on a tray.

"I don't know how you take it."

"Just sugar, thanks." He sweetened his coffee, took a sip and leaned back in his chair with an audible sigh. For once his gray eyes had lost their hard glint. "How are you and the children getting along?"

"Pretty well, I think," Cassie replied. Briefly, she outlined her daily routine. "We've been getting picture books from the library and planning excursions while the weather's nice."

Nick appeared to be interested, so she elaborated. "So far we've been to the aquarium down on the waterfront, several parks, the science center and a couple of museums. We're going to the zoo in Seattle next week."

Nick ate a bite of pie without comment. Maybe he regretted his impulsive invitation and wished she'd leave so he could get back to work.

The silence stretched between them as they ate, lessened only by the sound of a truck going by on the main road.

"You think Adam and Amanda like it here?" he asked abruptly.

Cassie pursed her lips while she pondered his question. She would have liked to tell him he should spend more time with them, but it wasn't her place.

Just that morning, Adam had asked if their mother would ever come to see them. Now she told Nick and his expression darkened.

"What did you say?"

"That she lived very far away, but I was sure she missed them a lot," Cassie replied truthfully. She'd been totally unprepared for the question and she'd fumbled for a moment at the time. What if Adam had asked why she didn't write or call? "Was that okay?"

He toyed with the handle of his coffee cup as he stared into its contents. "Yeah," he replied finally. "If they ask again, let me know."

"Of course," Cassie murmured. She wondered if the woman had bothered to contact him. If so, Nick hadn't felt the need to inform Cassie. No doubt he didn't think it was any of her business.

"We've been reading about baby animals, preparing for our trip to the zoo," she blurted, to distract him. "Adam has decided that he wants a baby elephant for a pet, or a snake, but Amanda thought a kitten might be nice."

"An elephant, huh? I don't think we're zoned for that."

The grounds were certainly roomy enough for a petting zoo, but Nick was probably right about the zoning.

"Children usually want something they can't have," she observed after the last bite of fluffy lime pie had melted on her tongue. "I always wanted a pony."

"And you didn't have one?"

Nick was looking at her attentively and she wondered what it would be like to have him interested in her as a woman. She could feel her cheeks bloom with color. No doubt it was a trick he used in business, to lull the opposition into a false sense of security.

"I grew up in a little bungalow in Ballard. Keeping a pony in the backyard would have been difficult."

"Did you have brothers and sisters?" he inquired.

"No, just my folks and me." For a moment, Cassie pictured her mother in the kitchen cooking dinner, her father coming home from work in the evening.

"Were you happy?"

Nick's question made her wonder about his childhood. All she knew was that he hadn't been born to money.

"Yes, I was happy," she admitted. "My father worked at the shipyard on Harbor Island and Mom kept house."

"Was your mom as pretty as you?"

Flustered, Cassie said, "She was much prettier." Even now her expression was often serene, unless she was trying to remember something that eluded her.

"What about you?" Cassie asked him, to banish the troubling image.

"What about me?" he echoed, the chill coming back to his eyes.

Oh, dear, now she'd done it. Then his face cleared and he stared down at his hands.

"My mother was a bookkeeper. You could say I grew up a latchkey kid before the term became popular."

"Was it just the two of you?" Curiosity overrode her sense of caution.

Nick's expression closed, No Trespassing signs going up. "Yeah, just me and Mom." He drained his coffee cup and set it back down—a gesture of finality. "So Amanda wanted a kitten," he said after he'd swallowed.

Relieved, Cassie followed his lead. "She wants a white one with blue eyes, just like in the book we've been reading. Its name is Snowball."

"Wouldn't Max hurt a kitten?" Nick asked. "Cats and dogs are natural enemies."

"Actually, Max gets along quite well with cats. The people who bred him had several and we used to have one, as well. She and Max were great buddies."

Nick didn't say any more as he began to gather up his papers. Instead, he put them in the briefcase and snapped it shut. "I've enjoyed this," he said as he got to his feet, "but now I'm afraid I've got some more work to do."

"Of course." At the abrupt dismissal, Cassie popped up from her chair and began loading their dessert dishes back onto the tray. "I'll take care of these and then I think I'll turn in."

Nick's expression was thoughtful as he bade her good-night, but he didn't say anything else as he headed in the direction of his office.

Cassie went back over their conversation while she loaded the dirty dishes into the dishwasher. It was clear the twins concerned him. So why didn't he spend more time with them? Even with his heavy schedule, he could at least look in on them once in a while. After all, she was only their nanny; they were Nick's own flesh and blood.

Two days after Nick's visit with Cassie, he arrived home much earlier than usual. He managed to make it up the stairs without being detected, following the sounds of childish laughter coming from the twins' room. Amanda still slept with Adam, so Cassie had suggested they move her bed in there and make the other room into a play area. Now their voices mingled with Cassie's quieter, deeper one.

For a moment he paused in the hallway, holding the large carton he'd picked up on the way home and wondering if it was the children he was doing this for or their nanny.

Afraid a noise might give him away and spoil his surprise, he pushed open the partially closed door and waited for someone to notice him.

Max raised his head, but he didn't bark. At least he'd figured out who the master of the house was, Nick thought dryly. Cassie was sitting cross-legged on the carpet, her back to Nick. Amanda leaned against her and Adam was sprawled on his stomach.

They were putting together a large, colorful jigsaw puzzle.

From where he stood, it was easy for Nick to see Adam's resemblance to his mother. Try as he might, he didn't think Amanda, with her light-brown hair and blue eyes, looked like either of them.

"Do you think Daddy will come see us when he gets home?" Adam asked as he turned a puzzle piece up and down, trying to fit it into a nearby space.

Nick's stomach clenched and he gripped the box tighter. Did Adam want him to?

"Your daddy works long hours," Cassie said quietly as she guided Adam's hand. "You know that he'd like to spend time with you, but he doesn't want to wake you when you're already asleep."

"I could stay up later," Adam suggested.

Cassie chuckled. "I don't think so."

"I wish you were our mommy," he grumbled, cuddling against her.

Her arm dropped to his shoulders. "You already have a mommy," she replied.

"She lives in Paris," Amanda volunteered.

"That's right, she lives in Paris." Cassie's voice was utterly patient. "And she loves you both very much, just as your daddy does."

"Do *you* love us?" Amanda asked.

Cassie reached out her free hand and pulled Amanda to her. "Oh, sweetie, you know I do."

For a moment, Nick imagined her reaching out to gather him into the little circle, her voice husky as she spoke his name, her smile soft and inviting. Then he shook his head to clear it. His gesture must have jiggled the box he was holding. From inside came a piercing wail.

"Meowow!"

Max got to his feet, tail wagging, and the three other heads swiveled toward him. Nick could feel a silly grin spread across his face. "Hi," he said, setting the box on the carpet. Another insistent cry came from its depths.

"Oh, hi. We didn't know you were here."

Cassie leaped to her feet. From her expression, Nick knew she was wondering how much he'd heard. The twins rushed at him like groupies who had spotted a rock star.

"What's in the box?" Adam demanded.

"What box?" Nick asked, stuffing his hands into the pockets of his slacks.

Adam giggled and pointed. "That box."

There was another meow.

"It sounds like a kitty," Amanda said in a hushed voice. Her gaze darted from the carton to Nick and back again. "Hi, Daddy," she added, clearly as an afterthought.

"Did you bring us a kitty?" Adam's eyes were round with excitement and he began jumping up and down.

Nick wondered why he hadn't thought of this sooner. Cassie was beaming with approval, her smile wide and her eyes glowing.

"Why don't you look inside?" Nick suggested. "But you have to be careful. We don't want to scare anyone."

Adam needed no second invitation. He started to yank at the flaps.

"Easy," Cassie murmured. "If it is a baby animal, it might be frightened. Remember how you felt when you first came here. Let's move slowly, okay?"

She sent Nick another smile of warm approval that made him feel ten feet tall.

Adam gave the flap another tentative tug. "Daddy, would you help us?"

At Adam's hopeful question, Nick had to swallow abruptly.

"Sure, Son, let me get that." He squatted and opened the box. Cassie, he noticed, was holding back Max, who appeared to be nearly as curious as the children were, his stub of a tail wagging nonstop.

"Look, Adam," Amanda cried, wonder in her voice. "Kitties! A black one for you and a white one for me." Her gaze darted to Nick. "They are for us, aren't they?"

Her sudden worry made him want to weep. A child her age shouldn't have known enough disappointment to put that look on her face. "Yes, sweetheart," he replied in a husky voice. "They're for you."

To his surprise, instead of immediately reaching for a kitten, Amanda rose and came over to him, putting her arms around his neck.

"Thank you," she whispered, tightening her grip ever so slightly.

Breathing deeply of her sweet scent, Nick enveloped her fragile body in a hug. Then he felt a touch as light as a butterfly's wing brush his cheek. Since Amanda had arrived, Nick had kissed her on several occasions. This was the first time she'd kissed him.

He had to blink away the sudden moisture that blurred his vision. Across the top of his daughter's head, his gaze met Cassie's. He wasn't sure, but he thought her eyes were moist, as well.

"Look!" Adam exclaimed. "He likes me." He was holding the black kitten. Its gold eyes wide, it was purring like a tiny motor and licking his face with its little pink tongue. Next to him, Amanda scooped the other kitten from the box.

"Careful," Cassie warned. "They're just babies, so hold them gently and don't squeeze."

"Like this?" Adam asked, demonstrating.

Cassie nodded. "That's right."

"What's its name?" Adam nuzzled the soft black fur with his chin.

"He doesn't have one yet. Perhaps you could pick one out," Nick suggested.

Adam's forehead wrinkled for a moment. "I'll name him Black Beauty," he said.

That made Nick laugh. "Perhaps you can call him 'Blackie' for short."

Adam grinned, snuggling the kitten against his cheek. "Okay. Hi, Blackie."

"Amanda, how do you like your kitten?" Cassie asked.

Amanda was cradling the tiny creature like a baby doll and tickling its creamy tummy, but the kitten didn't seem to mind.

"I'm going to call her 'Snowball,' because she has blue eyes like the kitty in the book we read," she decided.

Nick exchanged a glance with Cassie. "Works for me."

By the time Cassie and the twins got the kittens settled in the laundry room for the night and Cassie had tucked the kids in, it was past their bedtime. Nick had promised them the kittens could sleep in the bedroom as soon as he was certain they were big enough to find their own way to their litter box and back.

As Cassie pulled the door to their room shut, she heard the phone ring, but she knew Nick would answer it. He often got calls in the evening.

"I probably should have checked with you before I brought home the cats," he'd told her earlier. "I hope you aren't allergic. I was driving past a pet store and I remembered what you said yesterday, so I stopped. They sold me all the supplies and sent me to the animal shelter for the kittens. There were several litters to choose from."

That was the trouble. There were always too many kittens to choose from. She tried not to think about the fate of the ones that weren't chosen.

Starting down the staircase on her way to check on the kittens one last time, she could hear giggling coming from the twins' room. For a moment, she debated going back, and then she decided not to. Eventually, they'd calm down.

Before Cassie got to the bottom of the stairs, Nick appeared in the entry below. When he gazed up at her, the expression on his rugged face made a chill slide down her spine.

Her first thought was for the kittens. Had something happened?

"Cassie," he said softly, "someone from Woodlake House is on the phone. You can take it down here if you'd like."

Chapter Six

"I'm looking for Adele Hansen," Cassie told the emergency room nurse. "She was being brought in from Woodlake."

"Are you a relative?"

Cassie sucked in a deep breath, vaguely aware of Nick's hand on her shoulder. "I'm her daughter. How is she?"

"She's waiting for the doctor right now," the nurse said. "When he's done examining her, he'll be out to talk to you. While you're waiting, why don't you check with admissions? They may need some information from you."

"She has Alzheimer's," Cassie told her. "She may be confused and frightened."

The nurse's expression altered slightly. "We were told that. Someone will stay with her. Don't worry."

"Can I see her? Just for a minute?" Ever since

the phone call from the nursing home, a chill had weighed Cassie down like a huge rock on her chest.

"You can see her as soon as the doctor looks at her," the nurse said firmly. She glanced at Nick, who had insisted on driving Cassie to the Bellevue hospital. "Why don't you take her to the family lounge? The doctor will talk to you as soon as he's examined Mrs. Hansen."

"Good idea."

Nick took Cassie's arm and eased her in the direction the nurse had indicated. Cassie was barely aware of what he was doing until he guided her to a chair and stood over her protectively.

"Want some coffee?"

She shook her head, trying to think what she should do.

"Mom was fine when I saw her last Saturday," she said, rubbing her temple. "She didn't even have a cold and now they think she has pneumonia."

"She's the one you visit every weekend?" Nick asked.

Cassie looked up. He'd been so kind, telling Bull to call Mrs. Beagle and then insisting that Cassie let him bring her down here.

"Yes, I go every Saturday. You don't have to stay," she told him as she glanced at the big wall clock. "I'll probably be here for a while."

"All the more reason for me to wait with you," Nick replied, taking her hand and squeezing it. "Someone has to baby-sit the baby-sitter." He grinned and Cassie managed a wan smile in reply.

"You need to get some sleep," she argued. "It's late."

"I'm tough, but you look worn out. First my kids,

then two more mouths to feed and now this.'' He grimaced. ''Not that I'm trying to trivialize your mother's illness, you understand.''

It was Cassie's turn to squeeze the hand that still held hers. ''I know what you mean. Thank you.''

Behind them the double doors flew open and an emergency team wheeled in a man on a gurney. Cassie heard them say he'd been in a car accident. Almost immediately, he was hustled through another set of doors.

Across the lounge sat a young couple with a baby who cried incessantly. They didn't look old enough to be parents. The boy whispered something to the girl and then he leaped to his feet and began to pace.

''I'll go check on your mother's paperwork,'' Nick said. When he got back, he was holding a clipboard.

Cassie completed the form and handed it back to him. ''How much longer do you think we'll have to wait?'' she asked fretfully.

''Not too long.'' He patted her hand. ''Everything will work out, you'll see. How's her health in general?''

Cassie ran her fingers through her hair. No doubt she looked a fright. As soon as she'd grabbed her purse and Nick had roused Bull, they'd hurried down here. At least she'd still been dressed.

''Physically, Mom's in good shape,'' she replied. ''You heard me say she has Alzheimer's.''

''Yes. I'm sorry.''

Cassie blinked back fresh tears. ''We began to suspect something was wrong four years ago. She was diagnosed a few months later and she's been at Woodlake for almost two years now.''

''That must have been hard for you.'' Nick shifted

his hand to link his fingers with hers. "Do you have other family, anyone I should call?"

Cassie thought of Emma, her housekeeper, but there was no point in worrying her until there was real news to pass on. There was nothing Emma could do to help.

Cassie shook her head. "Daddy's gone and there's really no family except my aunt back East. I'll call her when I know something more. She's older and I don't want to upset her."

Every time a member of the medical staff appeared, Cassie sat up straighter and waited anxiously, but no one sought them out for almost a half hour. Finally, a young doctor walked toward them.

"Mrs. Wainright?" he asked.

When she got up, Nick stood, too, and slid a bracing arm around her shoulders. She was grateful for the bulwark of his strength. Without his support, she might have crumbled.

Quickly, the doctor told her that her mother's condition was serious and that she was being moved upstairs to critical care.

"We're doing everything we can for her, but we'll know more in the morning," he added. "You might as well go home. We'll call if there's any change."

Cassie shook her head. "I can't leave her."

The doctor's serious expression relaxed into a smile of understanding. "Why don't you head up to the third-floor lounge? Someone will let you know when she's settled and then you can look in on her for a minute."

"May I see her before she's moved?" Cassie asked. She needed the reassurance.

"Sure thing, but you can stay only a minute."

Her gaze sought Nick's. "Will you wait for me?"

"Of course I will." He gave her shoulders a squeeze before letting her go.

Moments later, Cassie gazed down at her mother's familiar face. Despite the oxygen, she appeared to be sleeping peacefully.

"I'm here," Cassie said, in case on some level her mother might hear her voice and understand. "You're going to be just fine."

An attendant came to stand by the bed. "We're transporting her now."

Cassie touched the back of her mother's hand. It felt cool. She bent and kissed the wrinkled cheek, aware of the harsh sound of her mother's breathing. "I'll see you soon."

When Cassie came back out, Nick was waiting for her. She ducked her head and her vision blurred. When he opened his arms, she walked into them without hesitating.

Hours later, Cassie felt someone shake her and her eyes flew open. Where was she?

She sat up on the short couch and glanced around, confused. Nick was peering down at her, his eyebrows bunched into a frown, and suddenly she remembered. They were at the hospital. She couldn't believe she'd fallen asleep.

"What time is it?" she asked.

"It's early yet." He nodded toward the doorway.

A different doctor was standing there, a stethoscope poking out of the pocket of his white jacket.

Cassie leaped to her feet, swaying dizzily from the sudden movement.

"Easy, honey." Nick reached out a hand to steady her.

"Mrs. Wainright?" the doctor asked. "Your mother's awake and she's asking for you."

"How is she?" Cassie was afraid to breathe.

His solemn expression softened. "She's doing much better. Another twenty-four hours and we'll know even more." He glanced at Nick. "She can have only one visitor at a time. I'm afraid your husband will have to wait here."

"Oh, he's not—" Cassie began.

"That's fine," Nick cut in, giving her elbow a squeeze. "I'll find us some coffee and meet you back here."

Cassie shook her head to clear it. "Okay." Meekly, she followed the doctor down the hall.

When she got back a few minutes later, she was still mopping up her tears. For some reason, they just refused to stop flowing.

"What happened?" Nick demanded, surging to his feet. "Is she worse?"

Cassie shook her head, unable to speak for fear she'd humiliate herself even further. When she'd regained a little of her control, she gasped, "No, she's doing okay." Cassie peered into his concerned face and smiled through her tears. "She knew me, that's all."

She didn't expect him to understand. No one could who hadn't been through it—watching a loved one slip away, her eyes growing blank, her forehead pleated into a puzzled frown as she tried to grasp memories that faded more each day.

Surprisingly, Nick seemed to sense how emotionally fragile Cassie was.

"You need some sleep," he told her gently as he handed her a paper cup of coffee. "Drink that and then let's go home. You can come back later."

"The children—" she began.

"Don't worry about them. What you need now is rest."

"Then I should go back to my house so I don't get in anyone's way," she replied. "I'll pick up Max and take my own car."

"I'm taking you home where I can keep an eye on you. Mrs. Beagle will stay with the twins." His tone allowed no room for arguing. Emotionally drained, she was barely aware that she'd agreed. Without rest, she'd be useless if her mother needed her.

"Thank you," she murmured as he led her to his car. Before he'd driven out of the parking lot, she was fast asleep.

Nick glanced at her repeatedly on the way to his house. Her eyes remained closed as her head lolled against the back of her seat. There were lavender smudges beneath the fringe of lashes, several shades darker than her hair. Her lips were slightly parted and her chest rose and fell with reassuring regularity.

He felt strangely content, watching over her as he drove down the expressway, surrounded by early-morning commuters. To the east, fingers of dawn streaked the darkness. The only thing that would have made him feel better would have been holding her in his arms.

Smothering a yawn, he finally pulled into the driveway and turned the key in the ignition. Before he could get around to open her door, she was awake and struggling with her seat belt.

As he guided her up the walk, Mrs. Beagle came out in a bathrobe, followed by Bull and the twins. They were wearing pajamas.

"How's your mother, dear?" she asked.

Nick spoke up. "Resting comfortably, which is what Cassie should be doing, as soon as she gets something to eat."

"I'll fix some scrambled eggs and toast." Bull ducked inside.

"I'll keep the children quiet," Mrs. Beagle volunteered. "You poor dear." She sent Cassie a sympathetic look.

Before Nick could stop them, the twins rushed forward to hug her legs.

"I'm sorry," Adam said, tipping back his head to look up at her.

"We hope your mom gets better," Amanda added.

"How are Blackie and Snowball?" Cassie asked.

Immediately, the children began talking excitedly, until Nick finally nudged them aside.

"She's been up all night," he explained. "For now, let her eat and have a nap. You can visit with her later." He glanced at Mrs. Beagle. "Will you stay for a while?"

"As long as you need me," she replied. "Come on, kids." She herded them back inside as Max pushed past her and shoved his muzzle into Cassie's hand, his tail wagging hesitantly.

"It's okay," she told him, patting his wide head. "I'm fine."

The dog seemed to understand; he followed Cassie inside and flopped down in the entry while Nick guided her to the stairs.

Bull poked his head out of the kitchen. "If you want to tuck her into bed, I'll bring a tray."

"Of course," Mrs. Beagle replied, beating Nick to the punch. "Come along, child."

Before he knew what was happening, she'd left Adam and Amanda with him and was herding Cassie upstairs.

When Cassie woke up, the twins were napping and Nick had gone to the office. He'd left instructions with Bull that he be notified as soon as she was ready to leave again. Not wanting to impose on him any more than she already had, Cassie updated her aunt and then she called Emma. Her old friend scolded her for not calling sooner and then promised to meet Cassie at the hospital.

By afternoon of the next day, her mother's health had turned the corner, and the doctor was cautiously optimistic that she would make a full recovery. She was in a regular room, Emma had just left and Cassie was preparing to do the same as soon as she called Aunt Ardith. No doubt Mrs. Beagle needed to be spelled with the children, as well. She had come back first thing this morning.

Moments later, Cassie walked away from the pay phone, still elated by the good news about her mother. Aunt Ardith had sounded relieved, also, but she was so far away and Cassie barely knew her. The sisters hadn't even seen each other for several years.

How Cassie wished there were someone else with whom to share the good news, someone who would truly understand that even though her mother seldom even knew her anymore, Cassie wasn't yet ready to let her go.

Glancing back at the bank of phones, she thought of her stepson, but then discarded the idea. He'd be at work, busy putting out brushfires. She had no close friends; since her marriage old chums had lost touch and she hadn't made new ones.

Jamming her hands into the pockets of her long cardigan, she ducked her head and crossed the lobby to the main entrance. Nick would have already left for his office; maybe she'd phone him when she got back to his house.

As she went through the automatic door, she looked up and saw him rushing toward her.

"How is she?" he called.

Suddenly, Cassie couldn't hold back a huge smile. "She's going to be fine, just fine."

"That's great!" Nick closed the space between them, wearing a big grin of his own.

Joy surged through her, and she couldn't remember why her feelings had been mixed just moments earlier. Tipping back her head, she laughed out loud as Nick reached her. Then, before she could think, he opened his arms wide and caught her in a big hug.

Cassie threw her arms around his neck.

"I'm so happy for you." He lifted her off the ground and swung her around in a circle. "I told you this would work out, didn't I? You just have to believe."

Without thinking, Cassie lifted her head from his shoulder as excitement and relief pumped through her. Nick was so close she could see smoky rings around the silver irises of his eyes. While she gazed up at him, his attention shifted to her mouth. His eyes narrowed and he lowered his head.

Still too filled with emotion to think clearly, Cassie met him halfway. It was only when she felt his lips on hers that she realized fully just what was happening. By then it was far too late.

Chapter Seven

The moment Nick felt Cassie responding to his kiss, he knew he was making a mistake—a mistake he didn't have the strength to back away from until he'd thoroughly tasted her mouth. Even then, she didn't struggle. It was up to him to break the contact and to drop his arms.

While he dragged a long breath into his burning lungs, she blinked, her eyes misty, her lips soft and slightly curved. Nick had to fight the urge to dip his head again. Instead, he tightened his hands on her upper arms as if he feared she'd lunge at him.

What he really expected was for her to slap him.

"I'm sorry," he said, letting her go. "I didn't mean—"

"It was my fault," she interrupted. "I was so happy about Mom—"

"I understand."

Several people stepped around them, and he realized they were blocking the hospital entrance. Two women sitting on a concrete planter, smoking cigarettes, were watching them with open interest. Nick glowered and one gave him a cheeky wink that made him grind his teeth.

"Come on." He grabbed Cassie's elbow and began hustling her toward the parking garage. "Have you eaten? Are you hungry?"

"I guess so," she admitted in a subdued voice, "but you should be at work. What are you doing here, anyway?"

"I decided to take a late lunch and I wondered if you'd join me." He needed to think about that kiss, but he sure as hell couldn't take the time now, not with her looking as though she might bolt at any moment. First he'd better do some damage control or he'd lose another nanny.

Beside him, Cassie slowed to a halt. "Did you want to go to the hospital cafeteria?" She pointed behind them. "The food's okay."

Nick stopped, too. "I know a better place and it isn't far from here. All right with you?"

She nodded and they began walking again. He'd parked close by and they decided to take both cars. When they got to the café and were seated in a cozy booth, he let out a sigh of relief. She wouldn't have come with him if she was planning to break her contract, would she?

Across from him, Cassie was still trying to sort through what had happened in front of the hospital. Had the kiss merely been his way of sharing her happiness in her mother's promising prognosis? As a good-luck gesture, it was certainly more effective than a high five or a thumbs-up.

While they perused the simple menus and ordered their meals, a grilled ham-and-cheese sandwich for him and a chicken salad for her, she tried to analyze whether he'd been affected by the kiss.

As far as she could tell, he hadn't.

So why were her lips still tingling from the pressure of his? Why did she want nothing more than to experience that stomach-dropping, pulse-pounding, mind-blowing sensation again?

Clearly, from the way he grinned at the cute waitress while he gave her their order, he had no such burning desire. Still, he did reach across the table and pat Cassie's hand as soon as the waitress poured their water and left.

"I'm glad for you," he said, "and for your mother. How long will she be in the hospital?"

"They're moving her back to Woodlake later today. I told her I'd try to come by this evening, but I don't know if she'll remember." A shiver of regret served to remind Cassie what was important. The last thing she needed right now was to be distracted from the complications in her life by a case of the hots for her boss.

Emma had told her just today that Walter still had no news about the IRS investigation. If it wasn't for what Nick was paying her, Cassie would be in serious financial trouble.

He seemed to understand she was on emotional overload, because he spent the rest of their lunchtime talking about other things: the Mariners' chances in the pennant race, the way the kittens were taking over the house, the report that had been on the news that morning about a local superferry running aground in heavy fog.

"I can't finish. I'll burst," Cassie said finally, sitting back in the booth.

Nick ate the last bite of his sandwich and pushed away his plate. "You don't eat enough."

"Sure I do." She swallowed the rest of her iced tea and blotted her mouth with her napkin.

"I never see you eat at home," he argued.

"That's because I take my meals with the children." Something he should try, she wanted to add. He still didn't spend as much time with them as he could.

"Do you want any dessert?" he offered.

She shook her head. "Thanks, but I didn't finish my lunch."

He crooked an eyebrow. "Does that mean you aren't allowed?"

"That just means I'm too full."

Nick glanced down at his hands. "How did you meet your husband?" he asked suddenly. "Family acquaintance?"

She smothered a dry chuckle with her hand. Robert hadn't cared that much to associate with her family, even after they became his inlaws. "No. I worked in a department store. One day I was sent to fill in at the designer boutique. Robert was shopping for a gift for his mother. I waited on him—he asked me to lunch." Cassie shrugged. "The rest, as they say, is history."

Nick's expression didn't alter, but she wondered whether he was judging her. She wanted to add that she'd loved her husband, but she didn't say it. Looking back, she wondered if she really had.

"Are you having any dessert?" she asked Nick, instead.

Nick looked at the menu, then closed it decisively. "I usually play basketball once or twice a week, but I skipped the last time, so I'd better pass on the calories, too."

"Do you play on a team?" she asked. That might explain how he stayed so fit.

"No." He signaled the waitress for the check, taking out his wallet. "A friend and I play a little one-on-one whenever we can get together."

She wondered what his friend was like—another successful businessman or professional?

"Bill's a buddy from my old neighborhood," Nick added, as if he could read her mind. "We wore out a few tennis shoes at the local playground and then we were both on the varsity team in high school."

"Did you play in college?" Cassie asked.

Nick left some bills on the table. "Between school and work, I didn't have time. Bill played intramural ball at the U."

"Well, it must be nice to have longtime friends," Cassie commented.

He studied her until she felt like squirming in her seat.

"Do you? Have old friends, I mean?" he asked.

She shook her head. "I'm afraid we lost touch when I married Robert."

Nick's mouth twisted. "I don't suppose you had a lot in common anymore."

She experienced a stab of annoyance at his superior tone. "I guess that was true, in a way. He was older—"

"And richer," Nick guessed.

"Yes, you're right. My father worked in the ship-yards. My neighborhood was decidedly blue collar." She frowned. He sounded as though he'd been burned. His wife? "They were the ones who ended the friendship, though, not me," she felt compelled to add in her own defense. "I tried to stay in touch." She had for a while, but then a busy social life and the responsibilities of being Robert's wife had taken over. She could have tried harder, though, refused to accept Beth's and Patty's excuses.

For a moment, Nick eyed her. "I'm sorry, I have no right to jump to conclusions."

"Sounds like experience talking," she remarked.

It was his turn to frown. "Maybe so. An experience I don't care to repeat."

Before Cassie could reply, he slid from the booth and stood up. "Shall we? I'd better get back to the office."

It was just as well. What could she say? Any response she made was bound to sound paranoid or hopelessly presumptuous. Just because he'd kissed her didn't mean he had any ideas beyond a little fun with the hired help. She could only pray he didn't think *she* had designs on him and was warning her off.

"I'm sorry, Mr. Kincaid, but Adam insisted on talking to you."

Nick's assistant looked slightly harassed as she interrupted his meeting with the president of a small software company Nick had been negotiating to buy.

Now he stood up, frustrated. It was obvious Harvey Rudd didn't trust Nick, but he had no idea how to get through to the other man. So far, the meeting had been spectacularly unproductive.

"That's okay," Nick told her. "We're nearly done here." Perhaps a little bluff would nudge Harvey in the right direction. "Send Adam in."

He'd offered to take the twins this morning so Cassie could visit her mother back at the nursing home and make sure she was settled in comfortably. At the time, Nick had forgotten about this meeting, so his assistant had been entertaining Adam and Amanda with coloring books sent over from the local drugstore.

Now Adam came into the office and glanced around with apparent interest. "Hi," he greeted Harvey Rudd with a small wave. "Who're you?"

Quickly, Nick introduced the unlikely pair, intending to ask Adam what he wanted and then end this meeting. He was disappointed it hadn't gone better. He knew an investor who was on the lookout for a company like Rudd's.

To Nick's surprise, Harvey leaned over to shake Adam's hand and began asking him questions. While Nick watched, Adam told the other man more in five minutes than Nick had learned in the whole time his children had been living with him.

"I have twins, too," Harvey volunteered, taking out his wallet. "Two sets." He pulled out a plastic holder stuffed with photos and proceeded to show them to both Adam and Nick.

Finally, Nick had a chance to ask Adam what he wanted that was so urgent.

Adam scratched his head. "I don't remember," he said. "I'm going to color a picture for Mr. Rudd."

As soon as he'd said goodbye to Harvey and left

the room, the other man turned to Nick with a gleam
of interest in his eye.

"Let's start over," he said. "Anyone who can
raise a boy like that might be able to look out for
my employees and handle my business the way I
want after all."

"Nickie, honey, if you didn't want to be with me,
why did you ask me out?"

The gorgeous redhead across the table from him
pouted prettily and batted her lashes, reminding him
of one reason he'd stopped calling her previously.
That and the almost assessing way she had of looking
him over, as if she were mentally tallying up the
price of his clothes and his haircut. He never knew
whether she was just making sure he was presentable
enough to serve as her escort or if she was trying to
analyze his net worth.

So far he and Margo had dated only casually. He
hadn't even tried to seduce her, at least not very hard.
Until he'd called her a few days ago, he hadn't seen
her since before his children had landed on his doorstep.

"I'm sorry," he told her now as he sipped his
brandy. "I guess I was thinking about work."

Margo's sullen expression relaxed into a dazzling
smile. She managed an art gallery and he suspected
her show of interest was a tool she'd perfected on
customers who came to the gallery.

"Problems?" she asked, leaning forward. "You
know you can talk to me about anything."

Admiring the view of her cleavage her change of
position afforded him, Nick wondered what she'd say
if he confessed that he found T-shirts and snug blue

jeans sexier than her revealing designer gown. His tastes, it seemed, were getting simpler.

"What I really need is to take you home and then stop by the office," he said, instead, making a sudden decision and tossing his napkin on the table. "If you're done with your drink, would you mind if we left?" He laid several bills on the check.

"I could go with you and then we could stop at my place for a nightcap," she suggested as she slid from the booth.

"Sorry, babe. I've got a lot of work to catch up on," he lied without a shred of remorse.

As he hustled her up the path to her condo a little while later, her eyes narrowed suspiciously. "Are you sure you aren't involved with someone else?" she demanded. "Not that I have any claims on you, of course, but I thought when you asked me to dinner that we were making some progress."

Nick hesitated at her front door, tempted to take the easy way out by saying he'd call her soon. Basically, Margo was a pretty, pleasant companion with a gorgeous figure; he didn't know why he wasn't interested. Perhaps he needed vitamins or more rest. Nevertheless, it wasn't her fault he wouldn't be seeing her again.

"No, I'm not involved with anyone," he admitted, rubbing his jaw.

Immediately, she brightened. "In that case," she purred, her long nails sinking into the fabric of his jacket sleeve, "would you like to come up for a little drink now? You can stop by your office afterward."

A short while later, Nick let himself quietly into his house. Although the hour was early for a Friday night, Adam and Amanda were undoubtedly fast asleep, the kittens curled into furry balls on their beds. The house was silent, so Cassie must have turned in early, as well.

Ignoring the surge of disappointment, Nick hefted the briefcase full of documents he'd picked up at work and debated whether to tackle the annual reports of the handful of companies he was interested in. Remembering his lack of interest in Margo and the suspicion that his libido was overtired, he tossed the briefcase on a nearby table, instead. Tomorrow would be soon enough.

Sometimes being truthful wasn't all it was cracked up to be, he thought ruefully as he switched off the downstairs lights. When he'd tried to explain to his date that he didn't think they had the right chemistry for a relationship, she'd called him several uncomplimentary names before she slammed her door in his face.

Now, as he crept up the stairs, trying not to wake anyone, he went back over the events of the evening and tried to figure out where he'd gone wrong.

He was clearing the top of the stairs when he spotted Cassie slipping from the twins' bedroom. She had on a long, clingy robe in a mouthwatering shade of peach. The fabric faithfully followed the sleek, graceful line of her back. Only a narrow belt bisected it before it skimmed over her hips, hinted at the rounded shape of her backside and ended in a narrow ruffle above the toes of her satin slippers.

Drawing the bedroom door nearly shut, she turned and gave Nick a glimpse of the feminine curves modestly covered by her robe. In less time than it took for her to blink in surprise, his libido proved it was far from exhausted.

"Oh!" Startled, Cassie pressed a hand to her mouth. "I didn't hear you come in." The tone of her whisper was accusing.

"I'm sorry." He was unable to take his eyes off her. "I was trying not to wake anyone."

"Aren't you home awfully early? I thought you had a date."

Bull must have told her. The man gossiped like an old woman.

"She developed a headache," Nick muttered, acutely aware of the children sleeping a few feet away. Lying was getting to be a habit.

Cassie glanced back at the open door and moved several steps down the hall. Without thinking, he followed her, watching the gentle sway of her hips as if he'd never seen a woman walk before.

"No, that's not right," he admitted as Cassie's scent, a teasing promise, floated back to him. "I took her home early. The date was a washout."

She glanced over her shoulder. "I'm sorry to hear it."

"Are you?" The real reason for the night's fiasco hit him like a bag of wet cement.

Cassie turned, frowning. "Pardon me?"

Nick crowded closer and she backed against the wall, angling her chin as she held his stare.

"You heard me," he whispered, voice hoarse. If she'd shown the slightest hint of nervousness, of resistance, he would have retreated. Instead, her eyes clouded and the tip of her tongue touched her full lower lip.

Nick's breath jammed in his chest and he pressed

his hands against the wall, fingers splayed, on either side of her. His heartbeat drummed in his ears like a runaway horse and hunger twisted through him, tight as coiled wire.

"What are you doing?" Her voice was shocked.

He tipped his head, gaze riveted to her mouth. "Do you want me to stop?"

"Not yet," she moaned, and her hands reached up to cradle his face. The kiss was a joint effort, her mouth lifting to his as he bent toward her, her lips parting as his tongue sought entrance, her body pressing against him as he leaned into her.

The floor beneath them could have fallen away, the ceiling crashed down on his head, the walls surrounding them burst into flame, and he wouldn't have ended the kiss.

Only the plea of a child's voice had them springing apart, gasping.

"What?" Nick demanded, spinning around. He expected to see a toddler staring up at them.

"It's Amanda." Cassie pushed past him. "She has nightmares."

"The hell you say!" His whisper was harsh. It was the first he'd heard about any nightmares.

Nick followed her into the bedroom and watched by the glow of the night-light while she soothed his little girl, kissed her flushed cheek and tucked her back in. He waited in the doorway as Cassie murmured words he couldn't make out, until Amanda's small hand sought the soft fur of her kitten and her eyes fluttered shut. Snowball blinked owlishly and then began to purr like a tiny, well-tuned motor.

Cassie asked a question, low, and Amanda's head bobbed in response. Then she turned over and hugged her pillow. With a finger to her lips, Cassie glanced up at Nick and slipped out the door.

Following her, he wondered how Adam could have slept through the whole incident. Except for the rise and fall of his small chest, the boy hadn't moved.

"Does that happen often?" Nick asked when they were safely back down the hall. "Her nightmares, I mean?"

"Not nearly as often as when I first came."

He held hard to his exasperation. "You didn't tell me."

Ignoring the stab of guilt, Cassie defended herself. "You're hardly ever around." Maybe she had painted a deliberately sunny picture, but she'd only been trying to foster his interest in his own children.

Now he rubbed a hand over his face. "You're right, of course. I'll try to do better."

His easy capitulation shocked her and she stared suspiciously. "Why now?"

He shrugged. "Why not?"

His flippancy annoyed her, but he was her boss and she had no choice but to accept his response. Pressing her lips together, she attempted to pass him, but his hand snaked out and he wrapped his fingers gently around her arm.

"I'm sorry," he said. "I only meant that you have a valid point and that I will try harder."

She managed a tiny smile. "That's good."

He looked away, dropping his hand, and then wrenched his gaze back to her. "It's just that I don't know how to act around them," he confessed on a rush of words. "They terrify me."

Now she did smile. "They're only four." When she saw he was serious, she patted his arm. The muscles were rigid with tension. "Just love them," she told him. "It's really pretty easy."

"I do." His voice was hoarse, his eyes smoky with emotion.

"Of course you do. It's okay to show them." She raised her hand to his cheek, felt the warmth against her palm. Then, in a rush, the emotions stirred in her by the kiss they'd shared flooded back. She swallowed hard as heat flowed through her like warm, sweet syrup.

As he watched her, Nick's eyes darkened, his face tightening with a predator's intensity. She wanted to snatch back her hand, but he covered it with his own, pressing her palm against his skin. She moaned, savoring the feel of him.

"Come to my room." The words were commanding, but the tone was pure entreaty.

Cassie's eyes flew back open. Pulling away, she shook her head. "I can't."

"Why not?"

After the way she'd kissed him, how could she possibly explain? Not that she felt obligated to fall into bed with him, but she had responded as if there was nothing she wanted more.

No wonder he looked confused.

"There are probably a dozen reasons it's a bad idea," she said.

"Give me one."

Cassie's gaze veered to his mouth and her mind went blank. "I have to go." Leaving him standing in the hall, she slipped back into her room, where Max poked up his head and then lowered it again with a gusty sigh.

Shutting the door softly, Cassie leaned back

against it, her heart galloping. Part of her wanted Nick to turn the knob and sweep her off her feet. The other part, the sensible part, breathed a sigh of relief when he didn't even try.

Nick glanced up when Cassie and the twins trooped into the kitchen the next morning. She looked as if she'd slept no better than he had. Good, he thought meanly as he drank his coffee. It served her right for being so tempting.

"Hi, Daddy!" Adam exclaimed. "Are you going to work today?"

Nick thought of what Cassie had said last night, pictured the reports he had to read and took a deep breath.

"Nah," he drawled. "I thought I'd go to the zoo in Seattle, instead. Know anyone who'd like to go with me?"

"Me, me!" Adam shouted, jumping up and down.

"Me, too," Amanda echoed, looking far less certain than did her brother.

Nick glanced at Cassie. "When are you leaving today?" He knew she still visited her mother every Saturday afternoon.

"Not until after lunch." Bull had taken the weekend off to go to some motorcycle race. Cassie was setting out bowls and cereal for the twins and didn't look up.

"Would you like to go with us?" Nick asked, surprising himself. No doubt she'd had enough of his children for one week. "You certainly don't have to, of course, if you've made other plans."

"Come with us, Cassie, please?" Adam asked her.

"Actually, that would be fun," she said slowly as

Amanda gripped her hand. "I've been looking forward to taking them."

He wondered if he should have kept his mouth shut and not interfered, but it was too late now. Both children were watching them expectantly.

Pushing back his chair, he went around Cassie to put his cup in the dishwasher. She shied away like a skittish horse, and he gritted his teeth. She hadn't been nearly so jumpy last night.

"I'll be in my office when you're ready." Grabbing the newspaper, he left the room before any of the questions he'd been turning over in his mind all night could leap from his mouth. Questions such as, what was wrong with two unattached adults enjoying each other's company when there was obviously a lot of attraction between them? He hadn't imagined her response to him.

Unfortunately he knew the answer to that question and to all those others without asking them. Complications, that was what. Cassie worked for him; it put her in a vulnerable position. He understood that. She was the last woman on the east side he should be lusting after.

And lust after her he did, he thought with a wry grin when she and the twins burst into his office a half hour later.

Cassie was wearing a red-and-white striped T-shirt and khaki shorts. Her legs seemed to go on forever. Nick was barely aware that his children were dressed in shorts and Ts, as well. The day was supposed to be unseasonably warm for the Puget Sound; he wondered if he should have changed his navy chinos for something cooler, also.

"Let's go, Daddy!" Adam exclaimed, dancing

around on one foot and almost crashing into the globe resting on a stand near the window.

Amanda had picked up a pen from his desk and was trying to scribble something on his blotter. Luckily, she hadn't removed the cap.

Nick abandoned the idea of keeping them waiting while he changed clothes.

"Okay, guys," he said, clapping his hands to get their attention. "We're outta here."

"Outta here," Amanda echoed.

And Nick felt a small hand burrow its way into his.

"The giraffes are way cool," Adam told Cassie, swinging their linked hands back and forth as the four of them walked down the path leading from the African Savannah exhibit toward the restaurant pavilion. "And the tigers and the monkeys."

"I like the elephants best, and the bears. Especially the baby cub." Amanda's voice drifted down from her perch on Nick's shoulders. She'd been nervous when he had first lifted her up, but Adam had ridden there before her and she'd surprised Cassie by requesting her own turn when he was done.

"What was your favorite?" she asked Cassie.

"I like the zebras and the flamingos."

"Who's ready for lunch?" Nick asked, his hands clamped around Amanda's knees.

Cassie had to smile at the enthusiastic replies. One would never guess the children had already eaten cotton candy and more peanuts than they'd shared with the pigeons begging shamelessly at every turn of the path.

Nick glanced at his watch and then looked at Cassie, hiking one eyebrow. "Okay if we stop for a bite and then I'll run you back home so you can pick up your car?"

He'd been unfailingly considerate and friendly during their tour, as if the night before had never happened. She wondered if he'd forgotten all about it, or had just lost interest after she'd turned him down.

"Fine," she replied with a brilliant smile.

"Good. McDonald's, here we come."

Adam let go of Cassie's hand and raced ahead until Nick called him back sharply.

"It's pretty crowded," he explained when Adam gave him a worried glance. "Stay with us, please."

For a moment, the boy looked mutinous as his lower lip jutted forward. Then his expression cleared while Cassie breathed a sigh of relief. Adam was a cheerful child, but he could be headstrong when he chose. Today he must have decided not to bother.

Moments later, they were seated at one of the many white plastic tables outside the food pavilion, eating burgers and fries as they talked about all the animals they'd visited that morning. Cassie was pleased the outing had been such a big success, especially since Nick was there.

While the children basked in his attention, Cassie sat back, nursing her strawberry shake and pretending they were a real family. She was still astounded that he'd acted so quickly on her suggestion he spend more time with the twins.

"Dammit, Adam!"

His voice sliced across her rosy daydream with all the subtlety of a chain saw.

"How could you be so clumsy?"

She looked around just in time to see Nick jump up from his chair, the front of his clothes soaked with iced tea. The rest of the tea and ice was spreading across the table in a widening puddle.

"I didn't mean to," Adam protested. "It was an accident."

After Nick excused himself to blot some of the excess moisture from his dripping clothes, leaving Cassie to dry Adam's tears, the ride back to the house was silent. So much for the happy family outing, she thought grimly, wishing she could chew Nick out for overreacting to what was basically normal behavior for a little boy. The sight of his set expression told her now wasn't the time for criticism, no matter how well meant. She kept sneaking glances his way, trying to think of something to break the silence that was growing more awkward with every mile.

Just as she was giving up hope, Nick glanced in the rearview mirror.

"I'm sorry, Son," he told Adam gruffly. "I overreacted and I shouldn't have. You didn't spill that iced tea on purpose—I know that. Will you forgive me for being such a jerk?"

Cassie beamed at Nick and then she turned to the back seat and winked at Adam.

"That's okay, Daddy," he replied gravely. "We all make mistakes."

Grinning, Nick slanted Cassie an amused look and then he eased the Mercedes through the light that had just turned green. "That's my boy," he said proudly.

Chapter Eight

When Cassie got back from her house the day after their visit to the zoo, a vase of daisies stood on the dresser in her bedroom.

"Did you two put the flowers in my room?" she asked Adam and Amanda when she found them on the patio, husking corn for dinner with Bull.

"There are flowers in your room?" Amanda asked. "What kind? Can we see?"

"They're daisies, and you can see them when we go upstairs later." Cassie glanced at Bull, but he only shrugged.

"That just leaves the kittens or the boss," he commented with a grin that showed the gap in his teeth. "I know who I'd pick, but you'll have to wait to ask. The cats are asleep and Nick's gone to play golf."

"I'm sure there's a logical explanation," Cassie

told him, her face flaming. Head held high, she fled back into the house.

Was Bull right? Had Nick brought her flowers? She didn't know what to think. Maybe he was just being nice, or perhaps he hadn't forgotten the kiss they'd shared any more than she had.

Dinner was nearly ready when Nick got home, so he hurried upstairs to shower and change. Bull was barbecuing chicken on the gas grill with the corn and russet potatoes. While the twins helped to set the picnic table out back, Cassie hovered in the hallway.

Finally she heard Nick's footsteps on the staircase. When he got to the bottom, she was waiting.

"Hi," he said, his gaze sweeping over her blouse and cotton skirt with obvious interest before it returned to her face. "Did you want to talk to me?" He'd changed into cutoffs and a short-sleeved shirt striped in blue and tan. His hair was wet from his shower and his cheeks were bronzed from being outside in the sun. "Is everything okay?"

Cassie remembered how solid he'd felt when he held her, and a shiver of reaction went through her. Trying to hide her nervousness, she nearly forgot what she'd intended to say. "I just wanted to thank you for the flowers."

Nick shifted his weight and shoved his hands in his pockets. "You're welcome." He grinned, deepening the lines around his mouth. "They reminded me of you."

"Why?" she asked, caught off guard by his remark.

He thought for a moment before he answered. "When I was a kid, I used to bring bouquets of weeds from the vacant lot to my mom—purple clover, yellow dandelions and those wild daisies.'' His grin faded. ''When I saw the daisies this morning, they made me think how lucky we all are that you're here. I just wanted you to know that you're appreciated.''

''I like being here,'' Cassie admitted softly. Good thing she hadn't assumed the flowers to be any kind of a more personal statement. As soon as she was alone, she'd have to think about the keen disappointment she felt at his explanation.

Nick's gray eyes studied her and then he propped one shoulder against the doorway. His partially unbuttoned shirt gaped.

''I'd never do anything to make you uncomfortable,'' he said, ''but I have to warn you, I haven't been able to get you out of my mind.''

His admission pleased Cassie, but she had no idea how to respond.

Nick straightened away from the wall. As if he sensed her confusion, he added, ''I didn't mean to embarrass you. I just wanted you to know that your job doesn't depend on anything but how you treat the twins.'' He glanced down at his feet, clad in leather sandals.

''I'm used to going after what I want,'' he continued in a gentler tone, ''but I won't push, at least not too hard.''

''I—I see,'' Cassie stammered, looking away in confusion. What was he telling her?

''Well, good,'' he said cheerfully. ''I'm glad we had this talk.''

''Me, too,'' she agreed with a helpless smile. ''Thank you again for the daisies.''

Up in her bedroom later that evening, she sat looking at the bouquet and remembering how he'd said he hadn't been able to stop thinking about her. She felt the same way; she just had no idea what to do about it.

"Cassie, something here for you," Bull shouted from the base of the stairs.

When she stepped out to the landing and glanced down curiously, he was holding an immense arrangement of orange, red and yellow tiger lilies in a copper vase.

Trying to hide her exasperated grin, she tripped down the stairs and took the card he held out.

"Perhaps you'd better put these in the dining room," she suggested, feeling the heat climb her cheeks. This was getting embarrassing. "I don't have any more space in my room."

"Good idea." Bull was trying hard not to look smug, and succeeding not at all. Behind him, a large spray of pink and white gladioli rested on the entry table. In the living room was a formal bouquet of red roses; the kitchen sported a purple African violet in a ceramic pot. A cluster of dried flowers graced the counter in the powder room. In Cassie's bedroom were arrangements of tulips in rainbow colors and a mixture of exotic-looking blooms whose names she didn't know, as well as the daisies, which were starting to wilt.

"Ain't ya gonna look at the card?" Bull asked.

"I'll read it later." It wasn't as if she didn't know who'd sent them.

Cassie wondered what Bull actually thought about this bizarre courtship ritual. Now, holding this card behind her, she gave him a weak smile and hurried back upstairs.

Slipping into her room, she took the card from the envelope and read it quickly: "Will you join me for dinner tonight?" No time, no location, just the same *N* slashed across the bottom that had been the only thing written on the previous cards. Was Nick finally ready to make his move?

The anticipation had been building inside her each day. She was ready for the next step, whatever it might be.

I'm used to going after what I want, he'd told her on Sunday. At the time, his bold statement had made her shiver with longing; the memory of it still did.

He wanted her.

Nick was a compelling man, but she still didn't know much about him. Why had his marriage failed? Why was he so wary of his own children? What drove him, and what, if anything, did he want from her, besides the obvious?

She had no answers. Tucking this latest card into her pocket to put with the others, she went back to the playroom to check on the twins. Tonight, after they were in bed, perhaps she'd finally have some answers.

"Any chance you could visit your mother on Friday this week instead of Saturday?" Nick asked that evening, over a meal of broiled salmon, wild rice and fresh asparagus.

Cassie sipped from her glass of chardonnay to give herself time to think. She'd changed from her usual pants and blouse to a casual dress sprinkled with flowers. So far the dinner that Bull had served before retreating to his private quarters as usual had been wonderful. The twins were in dreamland, the food was perfectly prepared and the wine a delicious accompaniment. Soft music played in the background. Nick had set out to be a charming and entertaining companion, sharing stories about his early years as if he were making a deliberate attempt to let her get to know him better.

Cassie had braced herself for a question at the end of the meal, which was completed with slices of huckleberry cheesecake. This, though, wasn't quite what she'd expected to hear.

"Why?" she asked suspiciously.

Nick swirled the wine in his glass, but didn't drink any. "I'd like to take you away for the weekend," he said quietly, his eyes locking with hers.

Cassie hesitated. Part of her had known this was what he'd been leading up to. She expected to be disappointed, but all she felt was elation. He wanted her. She wanted him. Wasn't that enough, for once in her life? Love hadn't made her happy; perhaps desire would, at least for a night or two.

"Okay," she whispered through stiff lips.

"What?" He looked thoroughly disconcerted.

"Did I give in too quickly?" she asked. "Were there some flowers you hadn't sent yet? I could probably hold out for another week if you'd rather."

Her answer must have finally sunk in, because he slid back his chair and came around the table. Enfolding her hand in his, he urged her to her feet.

His eyes blazed down into hers. "You won't change your mind?"

"I don't think so."

His intent expression relaxed into a smile. "At least you're honest. I can't ask for more than that."

Then he bent his head and kissed her lightly, breaking contact before she'd had nearly enough.

"Where are we going?" she asked, to lessen the sudden tension pulsating between them.

"A friend's been trying to loan me his cabin near Poulsbo. I think he wants me to buy the place from him. It's right on the sound and he gave me the key."

"I love being near salt water," she admitted.

His smile was gratifying. "Good. Bring your swimsuit and some sunscreen. It's supposed to be a nice weekend."

On the ferry to Kingston on the Olympic Peninsula, Nick kept glancing at Cassie as they stood at the railing. Another enclosed car ferry, similar to theirs, passed them on its way back across the sound to Edmonds.

Nick had meant what he'd told her; he went after what he wanted. When she'd agreed to go off for the weekend, he'd almost swallowed his teeth along with his carefully marshaled arguments. He'd even been prepared to offer to sleep in the other room, hoping to change her mind once they were at the cabin. Cassie's easy capitulation made him wonder now just what was on *her* agenda.

"Look at all the lovely houses along the beach!" she exclaimed as they approached the terminal in Kingston. Sunglasses shielded her eyes from the glare of the sun on the water and a light breeze tousled her pale-blond hair. The temperature was still cool, despite the promise of the cloudless blue sky overhead, and she was wearing white jeans and a long-sleeved red shirt.

Beneath their feet, the deck began to vibrate as the captain reversed the ferry's engines. On the car level below, the members of the crew would be preparing to dock, as the ˉbarnacle-covered pilings loomed closer on either side of the loading ramp.

"We'd better get back to the car." Nick dismissed his concerns for the time being and took Cassie's arm to escort her down the steep stairway.

In less than an hour they'd driven off the ferry, stopped at a small grocery store for supplies and pulled up behind a large cabin nestled in a grove of trees. As Cassie got out of Nick's Mercedes, balmy air greeted her. A breeze whispered through the leaves overhead, and beyond the house a gull cried. The setting was nearly perfect.

Cassie swallowed against the sudden dryness in her throat and reached back in the car for her overnight bag. After removing the two sacks of groceries from the trunk, Nick led the way across the cedar porch to the teal blue front door. Matching shutters adorned the windows below the shake roof. Hanging baskets spilling over with bright red and yellow begonias gave the cream-colored house a shot of color.

"What do you think?" Nick asked as he unlocked the door and stood aside.

Smile wavering only slightly, Cassie went inside and glanced around. A large room dominated by a stone fireplace and a wall of windows facing the water was flanked by a small kitchen with tiled counters and oak cabinets. Skylights added to the light, spacious feel of the place. Doors opening off the main room revealed a bathroom and a short hallway.

"It's pretty," Cassie replied as she set her bag on the round table and crossed to the sliding door that opened onto a wide deck. Hugging herself, she tried to control her sudden shiver.

Behind her, Nick set the grocery sacks on the counter and came over to wrap his arms around her.

"Cold?" he asked. "I could build a fire."

She shook her head. "I'm fine." She felt his breath against her neck as he tipped his head closer. When she didn't turn, he dropped his arms and straightened.

"Want to see the rest of the place? Herb said to make ourselves at home."

"Sure." With an effort, Cassie sucked in a deep breath and willed herself to relax. He wouldn't pounce on her, at least not right away. He'd brought her here, hadn't he, instead of dragging her down the hall to his bedroom back at his house?

She tried to recapture the courage that had enabled her to accept his offer in the first place, but failed as he picked up her bag and led the way through the double doors to what she guessed correctly was the master bedroom.

"Oh, how lovely." The room was paneled in some light wood, except for where a skylight was cut into the slanted ceiling. The floor was carpeted in a rich vanilla, and another set of sliders opened to the deck. Through the glass, Cassie could see a hot tub. Another fireplace, this one made from river rock, took up most of one wall. She did her best to ignore the king-sized bed that was positioned under the skylight, even when Nick dropped her bag on the quilted spread.

"There's a bathroom through here," he said after

he'd ducked into an alcove. "And a walk-in closet, if you want to hang anything up."

Silently, Cassie followed him back out of the room.

"Another bathroom." He pointed and then he opened the remaining door. "And a second bedroom." Smiling down at Cassie, he said, "I'll get my bag from the car."

Grateful for the moment's respite, she wandered in and out of the second, smaller bedroom. It, too, had a skylight, she noticed vaguely, and a double bed, but no fireplace and no slider to the outside, just a window that faced the grove of trees beyond the car.

"Hungry?" Nick asked when he came back in.

She noticed he'd tossed his bag on the couch.

"I could make some sandwiches." He began putting the food they'd bought away.

"I can do that." She was beginning to feel useless.

He glanced up and smiled. "Let me wait on you. You can help with dinner later." They'd bought steaks to barbecue, potatoes and salad fixings.

Cassie felt far too restless to sit still while he puttered in the kitchen.

"Can we take a walk before we eat?" she asked.

Nick must have heard the edge of desperation in her voice, because his head turned sharply.

"Sure we can." He put the meat and the cheese he'd unwrapped into the fridge, wiped his hands on a towel and crossed the room to stand in front of her. "Do you want to go back?" he asked in a slightly rougher voice.

It was the last thing Cassie had expected to hear. "I don't know." She pushed the hair off her forehead as she searched his face. "Are we making a mistake?"

His gaze flicked to her mouth before he replied. "I'm not. I'm afraid I can't answer for you, though. Why did you come with me?"

Unable to sustain his scrutiny, Cassie ducked her head. "I wanted to be with you," she admitted.

Nick sucked in a sharp breath. "You make it difficult to keep my hands off you." He gave her a crooked grin and took a step backward. "So, let's take that walk, have some lunch and not worry about the rest of the weekend, okay?"

His words relaxed her. Suddenly she realized she was famished. "Can we eat first and then take that walk?" she asked.

"I don't think I've slowed down this much since the kids arrived," Nick said as they wandered down the rocky beach, hand in hand. In his pockets were several rocks and shells Cassie had picked up and insisted on taking back for Adam and Amanda. He should have thought of that himself, but his entire attention had been centered on the woman at his side.

"Still no word from the IRS?" he asked her.

Cassie shook her head.

"I know how your husband operated," Nick admitted cautiously. "He didn't mind cutting corners." Had Cassie been aware of that?

She stopped and frowned up at him. "You mean the IRS might find evidence to support their suspicions?"

Nick realized he wasn't furthering his own cause by worrying her. "I don't know," he hedged. "But you must have some idea how he ran things."

"No, I'm afraid Robert didn't like bringing the office home, as he put it, and I didn't push." She gave a bitter laugh. "I was pretty naive about a lot of things."

"You mean about the woman he was with when he was killed?" Nick asked gently, leading her to a driftwood log and sitting down.

Cassie sat beside him and scooped up a handful of small pebbles. One by one, she tossed them in the water. "I guess you must think I'm pretty dumb."

Her husband must have been crazy, Nick thought. If she was his, he'd never look at another woman. The realization shook him to the core. Hadn't Janine taught him anything?

"No, I don't think you're dumb," he told her, watching the gulls flying overhead. "I don't understand men like Robert. I never cheated on my wife, nor have I ever two-timed any woman I was seeing. What's the point in that?"

He waited for her to make a sound of disbelief. Instead, she turned and searched his face. Their eyes met.

"Do you believe me?" he asked, and held his breath.

Cassie didn't even hesitate. "Yes," she said. "I do."

Smiling, Nick tipped up her chin with his hand.

"You're a beautiful woman," he said softly. "Inside and out. You'd be enough for any man. If you believe anything I say, believe that."

Cassie tried to pull away, but his fingers held her chin as he leaned closer.

Her lips were smooth and warm. He increased the pressure just a little and they parted for him. Her taste drew him in; her response heated his blood; her little murmur of pleased surprise sent every thought from his head. He was barely aware of her hand on his shoulder as he made love to her mouth.

Cassie could feel herself melting like candle wax in the sun. Her head was spinning when he pulled her to her feet, and she assumed he was going to hurry her back to the cabin. Instead, he wrapped his arms around her, holding her close. She could feel the rapid beat of his heart, or was it her own?

"Come on," he said after a minute. "It's too nice a day to waste."

To Cassie's surprise, he led her away from the cabin, farther down the beach.

"How's your mother doing?" he asked when she stopped to pick up a piece of green glass whose edges were worn smooth by water and sand.

"Physically, she's better." She dropped the glass into her pocket. Adam would want to know why its surface was scratched, its edges dulled.

Cassie didn't want to think about her mother's decline. It had been weeks since the last time a glimmer of recognition had lit the faded eyes, since a real smile had warmed her mouth. "I'm not ready to lose her," she confessed. "But each time I visit, she's drifted a little farther away."

Nick dropped her hand and put a comforting arm around her. "You never wanted children of your own?"

She stiffened and he looked at her curiously. It was a painful subject.

"I always wanted children." Perhaps a child would have mended the rift between Robert and her.

He'd been so disappointed when she'd failed to conceive.

"Then why—" Nick began.

"I can't have children." Perhaps the blunt words would help convince her of the truth she kept hoping was wrong.

Nick stopped and gazed at her, his expression grave. "Are you sure? Have you been tested?"

"Yes." There was a painful lump in her throat. "We tried for five years. Since Robert already had a son, I started seeing a fertility expert. The tests weren't conclusive, but I didn't get pregnant, either." Tears filled her eyes and she looked away.

"I didn't mean to bring up such a painful subject," Nick said, his voice heavy with regret. "I just assumed you weren't in any hurry to be tied down."

"You and your wife must have been excited about the twins," Cassie replied, searching for more shells as they walked. The beach was so rocky all she could find were broken pieces. "I don't know how either of you could bear giving them up."

"Her pregnancy wasn't planned," Nick said grimly. "She wasn't pleased. I thought she'd settle down after they were born, but she didn't. I was working long hours, building up the business, and she was bored. Neither of us gave them the attention they needed as babies. She left them with sitters. I was never home."

Cassie made a sound of understanding.

"Eventually, I hired a woman full-time. The next thing I knew, Janine had taken them with her to Europe and had divorced me."

"That's terrible," Cassie gasped. "You hadn't suspected there were problems?"

"I didn't see any, but I wasn't looking very hard," he admitted. "I didn't try to get them back—I just sent money." He rubbed a hand over his face. "I think now that's why she took them, so I'd keep paying until she found someone else willing to support her."

The poor man. No wonder he didn't seem to know how to treat his own children. They'd been used as pawns against him.

Before she could say anything, he began talking again.

"From what I heard, her latest boyfriend, some French count, didn't want them." Nick shrugged, but the muscles of his jaw were bunched with tension. "I got a call at work after she'd already put them on the plane. God knows what would have happened if I'd been away on a business trip. As it was, I had no time to prepare. You know the rest."

It was Cassie's turn to offer comfort, and she did. While she was hugging him, telling him what a good father he was, she realized what a good man he was, as well. Emotion flooded through her. It hadn't been lust that had driven her to accept his invitation to come away with him, but something much stronger.

Shaken, she dropped her arms and stepped away. He didn't seem to notice her sudden withdrawal, because he only slung an arm across her shoulders and dropped a kiss in her hair.

"Come on," he said. "This walk has given me an appetite and it will take a little time to start the coals and bake the potatoes. Let's head back."

Still attempting to sort out her feelings, Cassie could only nod and follow blindly, trying not to stumble over the bigger rocks, as he headed down the beach the way they had come.

Despite the enormity of her discovery, dinner was a pleasant success. Afterward they washed the dishes together. Then Nick poured them each a glass of wine and they sat on the deck, talking idly about everything and nothing, until twilight folded around them like a soft cloak. The only light came from two torches he'd lit and the glow from a lamp inside the house.

"Who was that woman you took out a couple of weeks ago?" Cassie asked, trying to keep her voice light. "Were you serious about her?" She knew she shouldn't ask, shouldn't sound possessive, but she couldn't help herself.

"That was a mistake," Nick replied. "We dated for a while last year, but it was never serious. I guess I was fighting my attraction to you, but the minute Margo opened the door, I knew it wouldn't work."

"Thank you for telling me," Cassie said, smiling in the darkness.

"Were you jealous?" he asked.

"Terribly."

He didn't say anything, but he got up and went inside. Cassie waited curiously, wondering if she'd been too honest. Then she heard soft music. He'd turned on the stereo she'd noticed in the living room.

"Would you like to dance?" he asked when he came back out and slid the screen closed again. Cassie had also noticed him fiddling with the hot tub when he thought she was busy in the kitchen earlier. Now she got to her feet with a smile on her face. She was ready to be seduced by the man she loved.

Several songs played while Nick held her in his

arms, and she began to relax. It was fully dark out and there was a cool but pleasant breeze blowing off the water. The last plaintive notes of a soothing instrumental drifted away and she felt his lips against her forehead.

"Cassie." His voice was slightly ragged.

She lifted her head. "Yes, Nick?"

"Will you come inside with me? I need you. I want to make you mine."

She reached up a hand and touched his cheek. "I want that, too." Her earlier nervousness had melted away, replaced by a burning desire to share with him everything she was feeling, even though she dared not put those feelings into words. She knew he didn't love her, but tonight that didn't matter. She was the woman he wanted to be with. For now, that had to be enough.

Instead of hustling her inside, Nick cupped her face in his hands and kissed her with heart-stopping thoroughness. His mouth was warm, worshipping, his tongue barely skimming her lips before he let her go. Cassie almost groaned with frustration.

"I've been thinking about this since I first saw you in the park," he whispered.

They were surrounded by the darkness and the night sounds, and it was as if they had retreated to their own little world.

"You were so worried that day," Cassie replied. "You looked frantic."

"And you looked like a fairy princess."

In the gloom, his expression was impossible to read. He lifted her hand to his lips and pressed a kiss to the palm. Then his fingers traced a path up her arms and curled possessively over her shoulders.

Cassie slid her arms around his neck and pressed close to him. Anticipation made her breathless; love gave her courage.

Before she could find her voice, Nick scooped her up and cradled her against his chest. She could feel his muscles flex as he shifted her and slid open the screen door. When they went inside, she saw a glow from the bedroom.

Candles! Apparently when he'd gone in to turn on the music, he'd made a small detour.

"Oh!" she exclaimed. "How pretty."

"A worthy setting for a princess," he murmured, letting her slide down his body until her feet touched the floor.

In the light from the candles on the dresser and the nightstands on either side of the bed, Cassie could see that he'd turned down the covers. The edge of the sheet was scalloped and trimmed with lace. The air was scented with vanilla, and soft music still drifted from the other room.

Before she could look any further, he drew her back into his arms and kissed her deeply. Then he set her away from him.

"Tell me you want this as much as I do," he urged her. "Or would you rather I slept in the other room? The last thing I want is to rush you."

Cassie had felt the strength of his reaction to her; she had an idea what the offer to wait must have cost him. Her response was to reach up and kiss him again.

A flame leaped between them. Fiercely, Nick caught her against him, his mouth hot and urgent. Wrapping her arms around him, Cassie met his passion with her own.

She'd never felt such hunger, such pure desire, as what Nick drew from her that night. The first time they came together, he tried to go slowly, but she refused to wait. Frantically, they stripped off each other's clothes and rolled across the wide bed. Nick's hands and mouth and tongue raced over her, seducing, maddening, tormenting. All the while the pleasure he so obviously found in her was more compelling than any aphrodisiac, more heady than any drug.

Finally, lovingly, he gave her what she craved, what he could no longer withhold. Together they soared.

Afterward, he lay on his back and held her close. Her head was pillowed on his shoulder. Just as she expected him to drift off to sleep, he cuddled her closer.

"You take my breath away," he whispered. "Are you all right?"

"Wonderful," she murmured, stroking a finger down his side.

He caught her hand in his. "Come on," he said, sitting up.

"Where?" Cool air hit her breasts, puckering her nipples.

Nick climbed from the bed, his magnificent body bare.

"Trust me." He opened the sliding door and she remembered the hot tub.

"Someone will see us," she hissed. "I'm naked."

He turned back, his grin boyish. "I noticed." He held out his hand.

Unable to deny him anything, Cassie skittered across the deck, her arms folded over her breasts. As soon as he removed the cover, she slid down into the water.

It felt heavenly, like a warm bath. Nick set a small cooler near the edge of the tub and opened the lid.

"Fruit juice," he explained as he filled two crystal goblets. "Alcohol and hot water don't mix well."

Cassie accepted the glass he handed her. Together, they drank, the cool juice trickling down her throat. When she put down her glass, she noticed two fluffy towels on the bench.

"You think of everything," she told him.

He set aside his juice and settled himself next to her with a contended sigh.

"Happy?" he asked.

All she could manage was a blissful murmur and a smile.

After they returned to the bedroom, Nick made love to her again. In the morning they showered together, lingering until the water ran cold and then hurrying out with squeals of laughter to pat each other dry with fluffy towels.

Over breakfast that he insisted on fixing and feeding her—warmed marionberry muffins, fresh cantaloupe, smoked ham and coffee—Cassie kept studying his face. What she saw there made her heart beat faster, her breath catch in her throat.

She'd hoped, if she ever fell in love again, to find a relationship based on trust and mutual respect. She hadn't dared wish for passion, as well. With Nick, she began to long for all three.

They spent the day in town, playing tourist. Nick picked out picture books of whales and sea creatures for the twins; Cassie got Bull a coffee mug with a mermaid painted on it, and her mother a tiny statue of a dolphin. They ate cracked crab at a tiny café built on pilings down on the waterfront and walked off the meal at the marina, oohing and aahing at the sailboats and cabin cruisers.

When Cassie's feet got tired and she began sending Nick lingering glances, his eyes darkened from silver to smoke and he hustled her back to the car. When they reached the cabin, he dropped the keys twice unlocking the door and they made it only as far as the couch before coming together, still partially clothed. Afterward, they lay back and grinned with lazy contentment.

"I hate to leave," Cassie admitted later when they loaded the car and Nick locked the cabin door.

"We'll come back," Nick promised.

"We can't," Cassie told him that night back at the house when he showed up in her bedroom doorway, his eyes heavy lidded with desire. "What if one of your children wakes up in the night or has a nightmare? How would I explain why you were here with me?"

"Then come to my room," he suggested.

Biting her lip, Cassie shook her head. "It would be worse if they came looking for me and I was gone. What would they think?"

From the carpet by her bed, Max watched the exchange as if he understood every word. Heaven only knows what she'd do with him, as well, Cassie thought, exasperated when Nick frowned.

He bowed his head and stood silently for a couple of moments as Cassie wondered if he was going to be unreasonable. Then his expression evened out and he came over to where she stood.

"I understand," he said. "I think I've got a solution, but I can't do anything about it until tomorrow. For tonight, I'll just have to miss you."

He kissed her thoroughly and it was easy to see he was reluctant to leave.

"Thanks for understanding," Cassie told him.

He glanced down at the prominent bulge in the front of his jeans.

"I just hope my idea works," he grumbled as he left the room, closing the door firmly behind him.

The next evening when Nick got home earlier than usual, he kissed the twins and then he gave Cassie a hug and a peck on the lips. Hot color splashed up her cheeks as the children stared.

"Why did you kiss her?" Adam asked. "You don't usually kiss Cassie."

"I like kissing her," Nick said with a smile. "She's a pretty lady. Don't you like to kiss her?"

Adam wiped the back of his hand across his mouth. "Ooh, gross," he said. "I kiss her because she's my nanny, not because she's a *girl*."

"You kiss me and I'm a girl," Amanda noted.

Nick and Cassie chuckled while Adam tried to think of a comeback.

"What have you got?" Adam asked, instead.

Cassie had noticed that Nick was carrying a bag from a local electronics store when he came in. Now he opened the box he'd taken out of it and held it down so the twins could see.

"It's an intercom," Nick explained. "One part goes in your room on the nightstand between your beds. The other two go in Cassie's room and mine. That way if you need us in the night, you don't have to get up in the dark—you just talk into the intercom and we'll hear you.''

"Cool," Adam said.

"Neat." Amanda reached for it. "Let me try."

"Let me!" Adam was used to being the leader.

"Ladies first." Nick showed her how to use it, then he showed Adam. While they were fiddling with the unit, his gaze met Cassie's over their heads and he winked.

The next weekend, Mrs. Beagle called to say she had a bad cold and couldn't baby-sit.

"I really need to visit Mother," Cassie told Nick. "I went early last weekend. I'm not sure if she'd miss me, but I really don't want to take the chance of upsetting her."

"You go ahead," Nick replied. "I'll watch the twins myself."

Relieved, Cassie kissed his cheek. "You're a doll. I'll go by the house afterward and then I'll come right back here."

Nick looked surprised and pleased. "You aren't going home for the weekend?"

"Not unless you want me to."

"Are you kidding?" His gaze was intense. "Hurry back."

As soon as Cassie had driven away, Nick took the twins into the backyard to play with a soft foam bat-and-ball set he'd bought earlier. Each time he pitched the ball, one of them would swing wildly until he managed to bounce it off the bat. Then the batter ran screaming to first base, which was really a folded towel, while Nick and the other twin gave chase.

He figured the game might not follow the rules very closely, but they were all getting a heck of a lot of exercise.

All went well for the first half hour. Even Bull had come out to watch and cheer them on. Then Adam managed to connect with the ball. He was so excited he ran straight to a corner of the yard that had been left in its natural state.

"Adam, come back here!" Nick exclaimed, growing exasperated. This was a much bigger workout than one-on-one with his friend, Bill Radich.

Adam glanced over his shoulder, laughing, and tripped on a vine. He crashed to the ground and immediately began screaming.

"Aw, come on, Son." Nick hurried over to where Adam lay, figuring on kissing a boo-boo or bandaging a scrape.

And then Nick saw the blood.

Chapter Nine

As Nick skidded to a stop and dropped to his knees, Adam's cries grew louder. Blood spurted from a deep cut on his arm. Apparently, he'd laid it open on a jagged piece of broken glass sticking out of the dirt.

He was losing too much blood.

"Bull, take Amanda. Call 911." Nick tore off his shirt and wadded it up.

Bull looked dumbstruck. Amanda's hands were pressed to her mouth and she was crying. "Is Adam okay?" "Is he okay?" she kept repeating.

"Bull! Get going!" Nick shouted as he pressed the makeshift bandage to Adam's arm. "Make that call."

Blinking, Bull came out of his trance.

"Come on," he told Amanda, scooping her up. "Your bro will be fine, but we gotta make a phone call.'' Carrying her awkwardly, he lumbered toward the house.

"Tell them to hurry." Nick held the bunched-up shirt to the cut.

With a last glance at Bull, Nick tried to give Adam a reassuring smile, but inside he was sick with fear. So much blood.

"It's okay," he chanted, trying desperately to remain calm. "It's okay. I know it must hurt like heck, but Daddy will take care of you."

By the time the paramedics arrived, Adam was sniffling quietly and Nick was drenched with sweat. In moments the man and woman stopped the bleeding, started an IV and loaded Adam into the emergency vehicle.

"Can you turn on the siren?" he asked as Nick scrambled into the back with him.

The paramedic winked. "Sure thing."

The next half hour went by in a blur for Nick. When they got to the hospital, he followed Adam into a cubicle, dealt with the paperwork someone handed him and held Adam's hand while a young doctor anesthetized his arm and stitched the cut.

"I can give blood if he needs it," Nick said. "I'm B positive."

A few moments later, the doctor looked up from the clipboard the nurse handed him.

"You can donate blood if you'd like," he said, "but this little fella doesn't need any. Good thing, too."

"What do you mean?" Nick asked.

The doctor wrote out a prescription and handed it to Nick. "Have this filled and give it to him twice a day with food. We typed his blood, just in case.

Adam must take after his mom. Yours doesn't match."

For a moment, Nick didn't feel anything. Then his stomach plummeted. He knew for a fact that Janine had the same blood type he did.

"Hi, honey. I'm so glad to see you," Adele Hansen said cheerfully when Cassie poked her head into her mother's room at the nursing home.

Cassie's eyes flooded with tears she had trouble blinking away as she bent to give the frail shoulders a quick but heartfelt hug. One look into her mother's eyes, so full of warmth and awareness, and Cassie realized that, for today at least, she was back.

"I'm glad to see you, too," she said sincerely.

Her mother's smile faltered and she leaned forward to pat Cassie's hand.

"I'm sorry," she whispered, her voice hoarse.

"I know. Don't blame yourself." After a brief struggle, Cassie managed a big smile. "You'll never guess what I've been doing."

It was so good to talk, really talk, to her mother that the time flew by. Only when the attendant brought in a dinner tray did Cassie realize how long she'd been at Woodlake.

"I didn't mean to talk your ear off," she apologized.

Her mother gave her a knowing look and then she made a face at the food on her tray.

"We have to visit when we get the chance. Now, tell me more about this boss of yours, Nick Kincaid. He sounds intriguing."

"Only if you promise to eat your dinner before it gets cold," Cassie replied.

A half hour later, it was clear her mother was growing tired. As she lay back on her bed, the mists of confusion began clouding her gaze.

"How's Robert?" she asked as Cassie put aside her tray. "You've hardly mentioned him today."

Willing herself to be content with the time they'd already shared, Cassie made a noncommittal reply and talked soothingly until she was sure her mother was asleep. Then, bending to kiss her cheek, she whispered, "I love you, Mama," before she slipped from the room.

Outside the door, she pulled in a deep, shaky breath. Her mother had been like her old self today; their visit was bittersweet.

Gathering her resolve, Cassie refused to let dark thoughts spoil the day. She could hardly wait to get back to Nick's and tell him about the visit. He might be annoyed that she'd been gone so long, but she knew he'd be pleased for her once he heard the reason.

When Cassie got back to Nick's house, she was stunned to find Bull and Amanda in the kitchen, making peanut butter cookies. Bull never spent time with the twins if he could help it. Nick had told her more than once that the ex-biker had no use for anyone under twenty-one.

"Hi," Amanda said. "Where's Max?"

"I left him at my house this time," Cassie replied. "Emma wanted to keep him with her. Where's Adam?"

"He got hurt."

"I'll tell her," Bull said gruffly. "You finish decorating the cookies."

He left Amanda pressing designs in the dough with the tines of a fork and he led Cassie from the room. As he described Adam's accident, she listened with growing horror.

"How is he?" she asked. "How's Nick?"

"Adam's gonna be fine. He'll have a cool scar."

"Is he in bed?" she asked.

"Yeah." Before Bull could say anything more, she raced up the stairs, expecting to find Nick keeping vigil by his son's side. Instead, Adam was alone, his bandaged arm white against the colored sheet as he shifted restlessly in his sleep. Cassie took a moment to make sure he wouldn't wake up, and then she went looking for Nick.

She glanced in his room and the master bath, but his suite was empty. Confused, she hurried back downstairs.

"Where's Nick?" she demanded when she reached the kitchen.

Bull slid the pan of cookies into the oven and removed the protective mitt from his hand. Turning his back on Amanda, he frowned at Cassie.

"He wants to be left alone."

"Nonsense. Where is he?" she insisted.

Moving closer, Bull lowered his voice. "He shut himself in his office and he left orders not to be disturbed unless Adam needed something. I think he blames himself for what happened."

"Oh, the poor man!" Cassie stalked down the hall, stopping in front of the closed office door. She knocked, but there was no response. Taking a deep breath, she turned the knob and went in. If Nick was feeling guilty about Adam's accident, she meant to disabuse him of that notion right now.

She was surprised to see him seated at his desk, surrounded by paperwork, as if nothing had happened, and more surprised to see a large crystal tumbler of amber liquid within easy reach of his hand. As far as Cassie knew, he seldom drank seriously. His hair looked as if he'd been raking his fingers through it and the expression in his eyes was unreadable.

She rushed over and gave him a hug he didn't return. He even seemed to stiffen at her touch. Was he angry that she hadn't been home? Did he blame her?

"I'm so sorry about Adam," she said, staring down at his averted face as she let him go. "I just checked on him and he's asleep. Is he really going to be all right?"

"Except for a scar the doctor said can be removed later."

Nick's voice was curiously flat. Perhaps he'd been so worried that his emotions had just shut down for a while. Some people did that when the situation was more than they could handle.

"How did it happen?" Bull had given her a sketchy description, but Cassie wanted to hear the story from Nick. Even more important, she needed to break through the invisible barrier he had erected around himself.

Before answering, he took a long drink from his glass. She could smell the whiskey fumes.

"We were playing in the backyard," he began, staring at the wall past her shoulder.

Cassie had to smile ruefully as he described the wild abandon of the baseball game. Nick had come a long way in shedding his reserve around the twins.

"He was so brave when the doctor stitched him up," he concluded, still without meeting her gaze.

"Like father, like son," Cassie said as she pressed a hand to his shoulder. She wondered how much he'd had to drink, but the nearby decanter looked almost full.

"Yeah." Nick's voice was dry. When he didn't respond to her touch, she swallowed her disappointment and leaned down so he had to look at her.

"I'm sorry I wasn't here," she said. "Watching the children is my responsibility. Perhaps if I'd—"

Nick shook his head vehemently. "Don't even think it. The piece of glass he cut himself on was partly buried in the dirt, had probably been right below the surface for years. Even the doctor in the emergency room told me these things happen when you have children."

"Thanks," she said, feeling a little better.

"How's your mother?" he asked abruptly.

Part of Cassie's earlier elation came surging back. "She knew me today." Sinking into a leather chair, she related part of their conversation.

Nick asked several questions, but then he began to fidget with his pen. "Do you want a drink?" he asked.

"No, thanks." She got to her feet. "You look tired," she told him, brushing back a strand of hair that had fallen across his forehead. "If you have work to finish, I'll go check on Adam again. Maybe I'll sit with him for a while."

Nick's attention had already shifted to the papers scattered across his desk. "Okay," he said absently. "I'll catch up with you later."

Before Cassie left the room, she looked back over

her shoulder, in time to see him drain his glass and reach for the decanter again. Either Adam's accident had shaken him up more than he was willing to admit, or the papers he was studying must be full of bad news, she thought, shutting the door quietly behind her.

"How long you gonna hole up in here with your bottle?" Bull demanded after he'd barged into Nick's office several hours later.

Nick glared and then, defiantly, he hoisted his glass and took another sip. "Why are you still up?"

Bull shrugged. "I was watching a movie and then I noticed the light under your door."

"Is Cassie in bed?"

"Hours ago," Bull replied. "Knowing her, she's got one eye shut and the other on the kid. You been up to check on him lately?"

"Since when do you concern yourself with the twins?" Nick drawled. As soon as the words were out, he knew he wasn't being fair. Feeling guilty, he swiveled his chair around so he didn't have to look at Bull's wounded expression. Dammit, this mess wasn't his fault.

"Why don't you just go to bed and let me get back to work?" The last thing Nick needed was his housekeeper prying into his business. His very personal business.

Not one to follow orders at the best of times, Bull dropped into the other chair, the leather creaking in protest. Nick turned back around in time to see him help himself to a drink.

"Adam's gonna be okay," Bull said, taking a sip.

"Hey, this stuff is a lot smoother than what you gave me for Christmas last year."

"I thought you were partial to that rotgut you buy." Nick realized he wasn't quite sober. Under the circumstances, who would blame him for wanting to blunt the edges of his consciousness?

The twins weren't his. Janine had played him for a fool.

"Did you come in here to discuss your Christmas present?" he asked Bull sarcastically.

Bull took another sip, letting the liquor roll around in his mouth before he swallowed. "Not exactly."

"Then why are you here?" The question sounded rude to Nick's ears. Good. He felt like being rude. Damn rude. When he thought of the gigantic joke that had been played on him, he almost laughed at his own naïveté.

"Ever find out you weren't as smart as you thought?" he asked Bull, who was watching him with a frown on his wide face.

"Never thought I was very smart to begin with," Bull replied with a derisive snort. He took another healthy slug of Nick's best Scotch. "So that's never been much of a problem. Is that why you're in here sulking?"

"I'm not sulking. And what I found out today is that I'm not the parent I thought I was."

"Hey, man," Bull said, leaning forward earnestly as the chair creaked again, "if you got a little upset with Adam out there in the backyard, it was just because you were scared. I 'bout lost my cookies when I saw all that blood. Don't beat yourself up over it."

Nick shook his head impatiently. He was still too

damn sober after all, when what he longed for was blessed oblivion. "The twins aren't mine."

"But you got custody, don't ya?"

Nick's head began to pound. "That's not what I meant. They aren't my kids."

Bull looked confused. "I don't understand. You're their old man."

Nick closed his eyes against the dull pain. "I'm not their father. They aren't my children. When their mother told me she was pregnant, I assumed they were mine. I didn't even question it. I married her. I paid support when she left and I gave the kids a home when she got tired of them. Nick Kincaid was such a stud they had to be his, right?" He poured more Scotch into his glass, spilling some, and took a long drink. "Wrong. I wonder who the hell their real father is," he mused, holding up the glass and studying the way the light shined through it.

"Is all this really true?" Bull asked.

Nick stared. "You think I'm making it up?"

"Well, no. I guess not."

"I don't want anyone else to know," Nick told him. "You got that?"

"Sure. Not even Cassie?"

"Especially not Cassie." The last thing he needed was her pity. "Swear to me you won't tell a soul."

Bull shrugged. "Yeah, you got it," he said after a moment. "I won't say anything. How'd you find out?"

"That's the irony," Nick drawled. "Today at the hospital I offered to give Adam blood. We aren't compatible."

Bull was clearly puzzled. "What does that prove?

I thought a kid just had to match one parent. He's probably got his old lady's blood.''

Nick set his glass down on the coaster, missing it the first time. ''Janine's blood type is the same as mine. That's why I remembered it. B positive.''

''There's no mistake?'' Bull asked. ''Hospitals screw up all the time. I remember hearing where one place cut off some dude's leg and it was the wrong one.'' He thought for a moment. ''Bummer.''

''I had them run the test again,'' Nick replied. ''Just to be sure. Remember, you don't breathe a word of this to anyone.''

''I gave you my word, didn't I?'' Bull growled. ''What you gonna do now?''

''Do?''

Bull got to his feet and poured the rest of his booze down his throat.

''About the kids. You gonna send them back to France or just call the state? I suppose they can find a foster home if she don't want 'em back.''

Nick's stomach fisted and the Scotch threatened to come back up. ''Are you crazy? They're just little children. None of this is their fault.''

Bull headed for the door. ''Well, it's up to you,'' he said over his shoulder as he set his empty glass down on a bookcase shelf. ''But if they aren't really yours, it changes everything, doesn't it?''

Nick sat without moving for a long time after Bull had left, the question hanging in the air like stale smoke.

Adam was still the same bright little boy who was curious about everything, Amanda the one whose shy smiles and butterfly kisses made Nick's heart turn over. How *would* his feelings toward them change, now that he knew the truth?

"Oh, my." Cassie stared at the little stick with disbelief and sat down hard on the edge of her bed. Taking a home pregnancy test had been more of a whim than anything else. She'd always been as regular as the swing of the pendulum on a grandfather's clock, but she'd only been playing at being concerned, having believed for so long that she was infertile. Robert had insisted she must be the one with the problem and she'd believed him. He already had a child.

She looked at the stick again. This was the second test she'd taken. Yesterday morning she hadn't even been worried when the first test had read positive. This one was a different brand and she wondered what the odds were of two false readings.

Astronomical, probably.

The negative tests she'd taken over the years when she hadn't been able to wait had always been heartbreakingly accurate.

The longer Cassie stared at the evidence that she was indeed with child, the mistier her eyes became. The wider her smile grew. She couldn't help herself. Maybe the timing wasn't great; maybe the government would take away everything else she owned, but they couldn't take this.

She wanted to laugh out loud, she wanted to hug herself and dance around the room. She wanted to hang over the balcony and shout the news at the top of her lungs.

She wanted to share the news with Nick. Beyond that, she was too excited to think. Briefly, she considered calling Emma, but Nick was the baby's father and he deserved to know before anyone else did.

Last night he'd never come to her room. She assumed he must have worked late and had not wanted to disturb her. She'd slept in this morning, but technically, it was her day off. Still, she wanted to check on Adam as soon as she was dressed. Humming to herself, Cassie turned on the water in the shower and slipped off her nightgown.

When she burst into the kitchen a half hour later, Nick was standing at the counter, drinking a tall glass of tomato juice. Bull was stuffing a small turkey. They both looked up when she came in.

Nick managed a smile, but he appeared tired and a little pale. Had he gotten any sleep?

"I'm making a tiger!" Adam exclaimed before anyone else had a chance to speak.

He was wearing a man's white T-shirt over his clothes and plastic wrap covered the bandage on his arm. His hands and wrists were smeared with orange finger paint. Amanda was similarly attired and the paint on her hands was blue. The table was covered with newspapers and more were spread out on the floor. The kittens were playing with a toy mouse in the far corner.

"How's the arm?" Cassie asked Adam.

He bent it experimentally. "Okay, I guess."

"I painted a fish." Amanda held up a square of butcher paper for Cassie to see. "Do you like it?"

She glanced at both pictures. "They're lovely." At any other time, she would have been happy to heap limitless praise on the art projects; today she was too full of her own news.

"Nick, could I speak to you alone?" she asked, unable to wait.

His faint smile faded completely. "Is there a problem?"

She wasn't sure how to respond. Would he look on this as a problem? She hoped not, but he already had two children. Did he want more? And how would he feel about having one with her? What if he demanded sole custody or didn't want her to have the baby at all? She pressed her palm to her stomach protectively. No way.

The direction of his gaze followed her hand. "Are you ill?"

She shook her head. No matter what happened, he had a right to know.

"I just need to talk to you," she repeated.

"I'll watch them." Bull's voice didn't even carry its usual martyred tone. He had to be aware of the altered relationship between Cassie and his boss. Neither had tried to keep it a secret; nor had they flaunted it. So far, Bull hadn't made any comments.

"Let's go upstairs."

Setting his glass on the counter, Nick gestured for her to precede him from the room. His manner was a little distant, but he was probably just exhausted, she reasoned. Perhaps it wasn't the best time to tell him her news, but it was too late to back out now.

She led him to his own bedroom and shut the door after he'd followed her inside. He leaned down to give her a brief but potent kiss, making her tremble with reaction, and then his eyebrows rose in silent inquiry.

"What's up?" he asked. "It sounded important.

Your mother isn't sick again, is she? I didn't hear the phone ring."

"It's nothing like that." Cassie tried to subdue the butterflies in her stomach and failed. The way they were flapping, they felt more like giant bats. Now that the moment was at hand, her mouth was dry and she was trembling. Maybe she'd acted too hastily, but she'd been waiting for so long to get pregnant that she'd gotten caught up in the excitement without thinking her situation through.

Now doubts began circling like buzzards.

"Well?" Nick prompted her. "Is it good news? I can't tell a thing from your expression. It changes every two seconds."

Cassie took a deep breath. "We're going to have a baby," she blurted.

For a moment, he didn't react at all; he merely stared. Then, to her disappointment, his expression iced over.

"You told me you couldn't get pregnant."

No wonder he seemed surprised.

"Apparently, I was wrong. I did tell you the tests I had weren't conclusive." Did he think she'd deliberately trapped him?

"Have you been to a doctor?"

"Well, no. I took two separate home pregnancy tests, though." Cassie's elation was evaporating, replaced by a shiver of foreboding. "I thought you'd want to know right away."

"You said 'we.'" His voice had grown as cold as the chill in his eyes. "Are you sure it's mine?"

It was Cassie's turn to stare, as a pain as sharp as the point of an icicle pierced her heart. Part of her had known he might not be as pleased as she was, but she'd never expected anything like this.

"Am I sure?" she echoed through lips gone stiff with hurt. "You're the only man I've been with since Robert died." She realized her voice had started to rise, so she took a deep, calming breath. "How can you think anything else?" she asked, praying his frozen demeanor would thaw and he'd sweep her into his arms, cover her face with kisses. Act as if he was happy about her news.

Something flickered in his eyes, but her own vision was too blurred by tears for her to interpret it. Could it be shame? If it was, it vanished as quickly as it had appeared. He remained silent, but the knuckles of the hand bunched at his side had grown white.

"I'll need proof," he finally rasped as he turned away.

"P-proof?" she stammered, dumbfounded. The happy scene she'd pictured so naively had turned into a nightmare. "Proof that I'm pregnant?"

He turned away, jamming his hands into his pockets. "Proof that the child is mine."

She realized she'd been clinging to the hope he was only reacting badly because she'd caught him by surprise, that at any moment he'd snap out of it. Now, though, that hope was fading.

"What kind of proof?" she asked, determined to keep her voice as steady as his, when, inside, she was falling apart.

He swung around to face her, his jaw bunched with tension. The eyes that she had seen softened by tenderness, darkened with passion, alight with laughter and caring, were now opaque, unreadable—as if he were the one who'd been hurt and needed to protect himself as best he could.

"Before I believe anything, I'll need to see the results of a paternity test."

It was more than she could do to stay in the room with him for one more moment. A sob rose in her throat, tearing at the soft tissue. Pressing a hand to her mouth, Cassie whirled and fled.

When Nick heard the door down the hall slam shut and the lock click into place, he finally relaxed his rigid stance and scrubbed one shaky hand over his face. A small doubt nagged him, but he shoved it aside. Maybe it was difficult to believe that Cassie was capable of the same deceit Janine had practiced with such lethal perfection, but he knew now he was far from infallible when it came to judging women and their capability to lie convincingly.

Cassie was in a desperate situation financially. What if she'd gotten bad news from the IRS? What if she had been with someone else, someone more interested in her money than in her? How could Nick take the chance again? He had to know, to be sure. Who would blame his caution, if the circumstances were known? Not that he would tell anyone; he regretted confiding in Bull. But neither would he play the fool a second time and risk being left holding the bag—or, in this case, the baby.

He heard a burst of childish laughter from the kitchen. A dull ache had taken up residence at the back of his head that went with the pounding in his temple. In his private bathroom, he leaned over the sink and splashed cold water on his face. Damn, but he had to get out of here. Without bothering to change his clothes, he hurried down the hall, resisting the urge to stop and press one ear to Cassie's closed door. Instead, he kept going down the stairs, then ducked into his office for his briefcase. Submerging himself in studies or work had always been an escape, one he needed today more than ever.

Shutting the office door behind him, he stepped over the black kitten that was rolling on the carpet and poked his head into the kitchen. "I'm leaving," he told Bull, holding up the briefcase. "I don't know when I'll be back."

"What about them?" Bull asked, glancing at the twins, who were still painting. Neither bothered to look up.

Today Nick didn't care how Bull felt about babysitting. His tolerance for the other man's eccentricities was at an all-time low. "Take care of them until Cassie comes down," he ordered.

Bull must have realized it was no time to show his independence. "Sure thing." His voice was as agreeable as if he were the model of household help.

Nick went out to the garage, but as he was about to get into his car, he hesitated. Had he been too hard on her? Probably so, but he hadn't been able to help himself. Briefly, he considered going back inside. Then he decided they both needed some time to cool off. Cassie would calm down; he would digest the news she'd given him and they'd talk.

Reassured, Nick kept going.

After she'd bathed her eyes with cold water, Cassie came downstairs in time to see Nick's car headed out the driveway. She was glad he'd left. She didn't want to face him again.

Later, when the twins were settled down for their naps, she slipped back into her room and dragged her tote bag from the closet. She was still packing, when she heard heavy footsteps on the stairs.

Cassie froze, wondering if Nick had come home again, but it was Bull who appeared in her doorway.

For a moment, he stared at her open tote bag.

"Going somewhere?" he asked.

Cassie knew it would be pointless to lie. It was bad enough she was leaving without giving some kind of notice.

"I'm quitting," she said shortly. "I was going to tell you when I came down. Sorry to leave you in the lurch, but something has come up—" Her lips began quivering and she pressed them together.

"What's happened?" Bull demanded.

Cassie merely shook her head.

Bull hitched up his pants. "Nick said he had no idea when he'd be home. Knowing him, you've got gobs of time. Why don't you come downstairs, have some iced tea?" he asked.

"Don't try to change my mind," Cassie told him. "I really have to leave right away."

"No one's gonna stop you. But I hate to let you drive away all upset." Bull waited until she looked up. "Come on," he coaxed. "I make great iced tea."

She knew her smile was weak, her eyes still puffy. "I know," she admitted. "Okay." It was easier than arguing, and she didn't have to tell him anything.

He got the story out of her before the iced tea in her glass was half-gone. When she thought about it, beneath the black leather and tattoos, Bull wasn't so different from Emma.

"You love him?" he asked gruffly, tugging on his earring.

Cassie thought for a moment. How could she love a man who'd acted the way Nick had?

"Yeah," she acknowledged, "but I'll get over him."

Bull shook his head. "I hate to hear you say that."

Cassie's eyes filled with tears and Bull shoved a napkin at her.

"He's not the person I thought he was."

"Nah, don't be talkin' like that." Bull shook a pudgy finger at her. "Nick's a good guy. He's just a little messed up right now."

"That's no excuse for what he said," Cassie replied. "There's nothing you can tell me that will make a difference."

"If I could tell you what I know, you'd understand." Bull's voice was mournful. "There's a good reason for the way he acted."

Cassie had been staring down at her hands, but now she jerked up her head. "What do you mean?" How could there be a good reason for his attitude?

Bull scratched the stubble on his double chin. "I can't exactly say."

"It wouldn't make any difference." She was certain nothing Bull could tell her would erase the pain of Nick's words.

Bull was adamant. "This would."

Despite her hurt, she was curious. "If you know something, you'd better spill it. Once I leave, it will be too late."

His eyes widened. "You wouldn't do something to the baby, would you?"

Cassie was shocked. "Of course not." She waited while Bull fidgeted with his iced-tea spoon.

"But I was sworn to secrecy," he whined. "I gave Nick my word. Couldn't you just trust me on this?"

Cassie slid back her chair. "You know I can't, but I understand your position. Thanks for the iced tea. Tell the twins goodbye for me, will you?"

"Aw, sit down." Bull shifted in the chair. "You can't ever let on that I told you, no matter what. I don't want Nick knowing I broke my word."

It was Cassie's turn to sigh. "Okay," she agreed. "I promise I won't tell."

Bull stared at his hands. "When Nick took Adam to the hospital, they checked his blood type."

"Nick's?" she asked.

Bull frowned heavily. "Adam's. Nick's not his real old man. It really threw him."

"What do you mean?" Cassie demanded.

Bull rolled his eyes. "He didn't father the twins," he explained with exaggerated patience. "Janine musta slept with somebody else and then she lied to him."

It was the last thing Cassie expected to hear. "He didn't suspect anything before yesterday?"

Bull shook his head, chins quivering. "Not that he ever let on. That's why he lost it when you told him you were knocked up. Déjà vu all over again, you know what I mean?"

Cassie frowned. "Yeah, I guess so." Bull had a point. Nick had acted so strangely last night. He must still have been reeling when she'd given him her news. She wasn't making excuses for him, but perhaps she'd reacted a little too hastily.

"You still leaving?" Bull asked.

She shook her head, picking up the tote bag and her purse. "Not right away," she replied as she headed for the staircase. "I need to think things through first."

Chapter Ten

While the children napped, Cassie paced the length of her room and back, trying to sort through what Bull had told her and the way Nick had acted earlier. Part of her was still hurt and furious that he could even think for a moment she'd been with anyone else. Part of her wanted to make excuses for him, to give him another chance, but she was afraid of being hurt again.

Robert had devastated her self-confidence. It hadn't been easy getting over his infidelity, but taking some control of her life had, at least in a small way, begun the healing process. Was she strong enough to get past the ugly words Nick had thrown at her? She loved him; she was having his child. Wasn't that worth some risk?

There were no easy answers. All Cassie could do was to hope her choice was the right one.

* * *

When Nick got home late that evening, he didn't know what to expect, but the one thing he hadn't counted on was finding Cassie curled up on top of his bed in a seductive black nightgown. She was sound asleep, her glorious hair spread across the pillow like a white-gold fan.

Warily, Nick approached her. Why was she here in his room? Perhaps she'd been waiting to chew him out and had fallen asleep. Didn't pregnant women tire easily? Janine certainly had. She'd complained constantly about fatigue, nausea and her ever expanding waistline.

While he stared down into Cassie's face, in repose as perfect as a porcelain mask, her eyelids finally quivered, and then they swept open, as if on some subconscious level she sensed his presence. To Nick's stunned surprise, her lips curved into a smile of welcome.

"I'm sorry I was so rough on you," he blurted. She looked so innocent lying there that he was tempted to confess everything.

Then Cassie reached up invitingly. "Later, sweetheart. We'll talk later."

For a long moment, Nick hesitated. How could he make love to her with so much still unresolved between them?

While he debated what to do, Cassie made a small sound, a moan, and desire surged through him. Unable to resist her silent invitation, he went into her waiting arms and submerged himself in her.

"I missed you," she breathed.

Her scent and the feel of her skin, as silken as the black nightgown she wore, seduced him, as did her voice in his ear. Wrapping his arms around her, he rolled onto his back so that she was gazing down at him.

"I'm a fool," he murmured brokenly.

She placed a finger across his lips. "Shhh, don't talk that way." Then she bent her head and nibbled at his ear, sending shivers of longing through him. He struggled to hang on to the shred of sanity that hadn't already gone up in flames.

"How are you feeling?" he asked. "I mean, are you sick? Are you tender anywhere? Should we wait?"

Her chuckle slid over him like a caress.

"For nine months?" she teased.

"If necessary." He'd probably die of longing, he thought, but he'd do his best if that was what she needed—what the baby needed.

Cassie felt him go still. Tilting back her head, she studied his face. "What's wrong?"

"You're having a baby."

"Mmm, that's right." She wished he'd said *they* were having a baby, but perhaps all he needed was a little time.

It wasn't easy for her to get past the pain he'd inflicted, but she had decided not to act impulsively. Love deserved a chance, at least, and this baby deserved a father.

Despite everything that had happened, she still wanted to tell Nick how much she loved him, but she knew he wasn't ready to hear the words. So she tried to show him, instead, with her hands and her mouth, with her touch and her response to his love-making.

Rolling again, Nick captured her beneath him. She

busied her hands with the buttons on his shirt as he caressed the sensitive curves exposed by the deep vee neckline of her nightie. When she had his shirt open, she smoothed her hands over his ribs and around to his wide, smooth back. She lifted her head to nibble at the firm muscles of his stomach and then she licked her way up to his flat male nipples. At the touch of her tongue, his nipples puckered into hard little points as he sucked in a ragged breath.

"I want you," he groaned as he stripped off his clothes.

Cassie watched him, mesmerized by his male beauty. His eyes dark with emotion, he lifted the hem of her nightie and slipped it over her head.

Cassie lay back down as he looked at her, his gaze missing nothing. When he splayed his fingers across her flat stomach, she pressed her hand over his. He didn't say anything, but the bemused expression in his eyes was enough for now.

Soon his caresses took on a new urgency as her own blood heated, her body yearning for fulfillment. His fingers and then his mouth probed intimately, making her gasp with reaction. Before she could collect her scattered thoughts, he claimed her with an intensity that left her breathless.

"Cassie," he moaned, eyes squeezed shut, teeth bared. "Sweet, sweet Cassie."

After that, there were no more words, only feelings, only passion. Only—on Cassie's part at least— love.

She awoke later to the sound of Adam on the intercom, calling her.

"I'll go," Nick said before she could stir. She mumbled a protest, but he was already belting his robe. Leaning down, he kissed her lightly and then touched the tip of her nose with his finger. "You need your rest."

Before she fell back asleep, she wondered what the heck she was supposed to tell him if he thought to ask why she'd forgiven him so easily.

Nick didn't put the question into words, but it ate at him. He'd been a total bastard to her and she'd apparently shrugged off the incident like some minor misunderstanding. Why?

Only a woman in love or a desperate one would overlook the kind of accusation he'd made. Cassie certainly acted as though she found him attractive enough, but love?

More likely she was desperate, or she wouldn't have gone to work for him. Some women would do nearly anything for wealth, security and power, or a man who could furnish all three.

Was Cassie one of those women?

For the next couple of weeks, he watched her carefully. She seemed happy, loving, unconcerned by his lack of commitment to her and the baby. The more he looked for some small hint of harbored resentment toward him, the less he found. It was as if she'd forgotten the ugly scene had ever happened. The less evidence he found, the more his own suspicion grew. He'd be damned if a woman would ever play him for a fool again, even Cassie.

He suggested she move her things into his bedroom and she agreed. The twins adapted to the change without comment. Every night Nick made love to her. Every morning he woke up with her in his arms. He was falling fast and his own feelings terrified him.

If Cassie lost her fortune, how could he ever know if it was he or his money that attracted her? As his feelings for her grew, so did his obsession. If he were to lose everything else, would he lose her, as well?

One morning when he was reading in the newspaper about an acquaintance who'd gone through bankruptcy and then a bitter divorce, Nick had an idea. The more he thought about it, the more tempted he was to get at the truth once and for all.

"You're nuts," Bull said bluntly, chopping hard-boiled eggs for the potato salad he was making. They were having a picnic in the backyard that afternoon—cold chicken, fruit, chips, and chocolate cupcakes for dessert. Adam and Amanda had chosen the menu, except for the potato salad Nick had requested.

"I just want to eliminate the possibility, that's all," Nick argued. "If you're right about her, she'll stay with me. If not, she'll bolt, especially if the IRS rules in her favor. If she stands by me, I'll eventually tell her I've managed to save the company from financial ruin. She'll never suspect it was all a ruse, but I'll know it's me she's attracted to and not my money." He spread his hands wide. "What could possibly go wrong?"

Bull turned and waved the heavy cleaver he'd been using under Nick's nose until he'd backed hastily away. "I bet Bill Gates never put his wife through any kind of harebrained test like this," he grumbled. "The whole thing's gonna blow up in your face and Cassie will be the one who gets hurt the most. You're lucky she forgave you for the last time your brain went dead. Don't push it.''

Nick wondered how Bull knew about that unfortunate incident. Had he overheard them, or had Cassie told him? Nick's housekeeper was certainly getting in touch with his tender side. First he'd taken a belated interest in the twins; now he was apparently fielding confidences from their nanny.

Jealousy sizzled through Nick like a splatter of hot grease.

''I'll be careful,'' he insisted. ''No one will be hurt and my doubts will be laid to rest, once and for all.''

In reply, Bull began chopping celery as if he were beheading an army of rival bikers. All the while, he muttered something Nick figured he didn't need to hear.

Several days later, Nick had a chance to put his plan into effect. When he came dragging in from work after a gruesome afternoon spent trying to salvage a minor takeover from going in the toilet, Cassie was waiting for him.

''How was your day?'' she asked after he'd swept her into his arms and kissed her with a thoroughness that left him aroused and her noticeably short of breath.

Nick searched her gaze. She certainly looked sincere, but he just couldn't tell anymore. Was it he who really attracted her, or the number of zeros in his bank balance? Paranoid or not, he needed to know.

Forcing a smile that was grim around the edges, he replied, ''Uh, my day was okay, I guess. How was yours?''

Her smile wavered, shadowed now with concern. "There's something you aren't telling me."

He wasn't that good an actor, but the strength of her perception astounded him. This was going to be easier than he'd hoped.

"We'll talk after we eat, okay?" Cassie had gotten in the habit of having a light meal with the children and then joining him later. On the infrequent occasions when he got home early, they all ate together.

Now Nick washed up while she set out the salad and chilled roast beef Bull had left for him. As he ate and she moved her food around on her plate with her fork, he could almost feel her worry—but was it for him or merely for her own tenuous situation?

Finally, he shoved his plate aside and tried to appear properly gloomy. "I'm in trouble," he confessed with proper gravity. "Big trouble."

Cassie's eyes widened and she slid back her chair. Rushing around the table, she hugged him to her. "I had a feeling it was something like that. Tell me about it."

With his head cradled against her breasts, it was difficult for Nick to think at all, let alone to recite the carefully chosen words he'd rehearsed earlier. No sooner were the hints of disaster out than she let him go abruptly. His heart lurched. Was she going to betray herself so quickly? Now that he'd set the wheels in motion, he was astounded how much the possibility hurt.

Cassie sat back down with a plop, her face a picture of distress. "Oh, dear," she wailed, "I wish my own situation weren't such a mess. If I had any assets I could put my hands on, I could help you out."

At her impassioned words, guilt and shame pierced

Nick's heart like a sword of betrayal. He didn't know how to respond. Gathering himself, he managed to say, "Thank you for the thought, honey, but I wouldn't want you to go down with me."

"Is it that bad?" she whispered, clearly horrified.

Beginning to feel like a first-class rat, he nodded. "I'm afraid it could be." Covering his face with his hands, he managed to peek between two fingers. She was chewing on her lower lip thoughtfully.

Then she brightened. "No matter what happens, you'll still have the children," she told him. "And me, of course." Her cheeks went pink and she lowered her gaze. "If that's what you want, I mean."

Either she was the most precious woman in the world or a damn good actress, he thought cynically. He'd never wanted so much to be wrong in his suspicions. If only his gut weren't telling him she was too good to be real.

He reached out a hand to hers where it lay on the table. "You're right, of course. Even if we have nothing, if we end up in a tiny apartment or a little trailer with the twins, we'll still have each other."

Her eyes flickered and he wondered if he'd gone too far. "I'm glad you feel that way," was all she said.

A couple of afternoons later, Nick left the office early. When he walked into the kitchen, Cassie was seated at the table, holding a pair of scissors and several tattered flyers.

"What are you doing?" he asked curiously as she got up to greet him.

"I'm clipping coupons," she replied, beaming. "I know it's only a drop in the bucket, but we can save

quite a bit on our groceries if we watch the ads, plan
the menu according to what's on sale and stop having
everything delivered.''

From his place in front of the stove, Bull sent Nick
a black frown. ''She's been coming up with all kinds
of ways to save,'' he growled.

''Great.'' Nick didn't know what to think. By that
evening when Cassie had joined him in his room,
rubbing the knots from his shoulders and giving him
a pep talk about not getting discouraged by life's
setbacks, he was even more confused. Wasn't this
supposed to be when she started making plans to
desert the sinking ship? She seemed more intent on
plugging the holes with grocery store sale flyers.

Next, she suggested that he turn in his leased Mercedes and look for an economical used car, instead.
It wasn't easy convincing her he needed to keep up
his facade of success or the buzzards would start circling. Then she began asking pointed questions about
his money problems.

''Why do you want to know?'' he asked, more
wary than ever as they cuddled in his bed after making love. Nick's head was still spinning from the way
she had come apart in his arms moments before. She
made him feel ten feet tall. Suddenly he wondered if
boosting his ego was part of her ten-point plan to
buoy his spirits while she overhauled his budget.

Conversely, his ego sank to a new low.

Cassie reached out a hand to caress his cheek. ''I
know it will take a lot more than these little things
to make a real difference, so I thought perhaps Miles
could come up with some ideas to help you,'' she
replied with a smile.

Nick jackknifed to a sitting position. ''You can't

tell your stepson!'' Real panic coursed through Nick's veins. If word got out that his company was in trouble, phony or not, he could end up in an extremely vulnerable situation. The investment group he was assembling to buy a cellular telephone manufacturing company rumored to be in financial trouble of its own would fall apart faster than Adam could demolish a tower made of Tinkertoys.

''Why can't I? Miles is pretty sharp. Before his death, Robert taught him everything he knew.''

''And look at the situation Robert left his own company in,'' Nick retaliated, his heart still racing at the threat of a leak.

Cassie looked hurt, so he grabbed her hands. ''Sweetheart, gossip about my difficulties could only hasten my company's demise.''

''Miles wouldn't say anything.''

''He might slip,'' Nick replied.

Finally he convinced her not to say anything to her stepson.

''Don't worry, I won't breathe a word to anyone,'' she promised, leaning forward to plant a kiss on Nick's lips. ''We'll just have to come up with something ourselves, won't we?''

Bull spent the next morning pummeling bread dough and wishing he could pack his duffel bag, climb on his bike and ride into the sunset. He'd never seen two people more suited to each other than his boss and Cassie Wainright, but he could hardly believe the mess they'd made of things. Cassie was busy economizing the place to death—she'd even looked over his grocery order and slashed almost a third of it. Nick swung between suspicion, sappy

lovesickness and guilt over his deceit like a monkey
swinging on a jungle vine.

Hell's bells, Bull grumbled as he folded the dough
over and pounded it down again. What was a sane
man supposed to do when he was surrounded by all
this damn romantic craziness, anyway?

If he told Cassie about Nick's stupid little scheme
to test her loyalty, she'd tear out of there as fast as
if Bull's own former biker buddies were on her tail.
Nick would can him for spilling the beans. Neither
could he admit to Nick that he'd broken his word
and told Cassie about the twins.

Talk about being stuck between a rock and a hard
place.

Bull rolled his eyes and sprinkled flour on the
dough. Any fool could see Cassie had a major case
of the hots for her boss. Bull had done his damnedest
to convince Nick of that. Did he listen? Hell, no.
He'd rather think the worst and make everyone miserable.

Bull was sure gonna be miserable if he had to do
the grocery shopping in person instead of just picking
up the phone. Some of the single women who hung
out at the local market were way scarier than the
biker babes he'd known in the past.

Besides, he hated to see either Nick or Cassie get
hurt. Nick had been more than just a boss; if he
hadn't hired Bull, he'd be either dead or in prison by
now.

This was by far the best gig he'd ever had. If he
lost it, he'd be lucky to get a job as a professional
wrestler, throwing matches to guys with fake tans
and bleached hair in high-school gyms in little back-
water towns for twenty bucks a night, or working as

a part-time bouncer in some grade Z strip club full of real weirdos and deviants.

Bull scratched his chest right next to the silver ring that pierced his nipple. All this anxiety because he'd tried to help two people who couldn't figure out how they really felt about each other.

Hefting the slab of pumpernickel into the air, he flipped it over and slammed it back down on the counter before he remembered it was only bread dough, not the member of a rival biker gang who'd infringed on Devil's Spawn turf. The way he was treating the damn dough it would end up so tough it wouldn't even make decent pita bread.

By the time he'd filled his baking pans and put the whole batch in the oven, he was no closer to a solution than before. He just had one hell of a headache from the strain of too much thinking.

Bull was wiping flour off the kitchen counter when Nick came in the back door. He was whistling. Every note was like a red-hot ice pick stabbing holes through the backs of Bull's eyes.

Nick took one look at him and stopped in his tracks. "Migraine?" he asked sympathetically.

Bull could only nod with extreme care. Even that slight movement hurt. The pain was getting intense; a cold sweat was breaking out all over his body and his stomach was doing three-sixties. He needed darkness, quiet and sleep, not necessarily in that order. A clear conscience wouldn't have hurt, either.

"Go lie down," Nick told him. "We can manage without you for a few hours."

"Thanks," Bull grunted and then he remembered the bread. "Uh, can you have Cassie turn out the loaves when the timer goes off?'' he asked. ''She'll know what to do with them.''

''Sure.'' Nick reached in his pocket and pulled out a small velvet box. ''Before you go, I just wanted to show you what I picked up this morning. What do you think?''

He flipped open the lid and Bull stared at the egg-shaped rock glittering up at him like a headlight surrounded by only slightly smaller rocks. Bull could only groan and squeeze his eyes shut.

''Too gaudy?'' Nick asked. ''I don't want her thinking I overspent, since I'm supposed to be going broke.''

Bull put a hand to his forehead. ''Why are you doing this now?'' He had a bad feeling that it was all part of Nick's ''test.''

''I'm going to tell her my company just lost out on a major deal that should bankrupt me,'' Nick confided in a low voice. ''If she still accepts my proposal, I'll know she loves me for myself and not the fortune she thinks I'm losing. If she puts me off, well, then I guess I've had a narrow escape, haven't I?''

The pain in Bull's head immediately shot off the scale.

''I'm so sorry, baby,'' Cassie told Nick. She wanted to put her arms around him. He looked so alone. They were standing at the window of a private alcove in a fancy restaurant on the Seattle waterfront. ''I wish there were something I could do,'' she added. ''I feel so helpless.'' He had just confided that it didn't look good for his company. Because of a dramatic shift in the market, a major undertaking he'd been involved in was about to go sour and he faced bankruptcy.

"I know, honey," he replied somberly. "And I appreciate your concern—I really do—but these things happen."

He was so brave. Her heart ached for him. Everything he'd worked so hard for was about to slip away from him and she wanted to weep.

On the other side of the glass, the lingering sunset had streaked the sky with lavender, coral and peach, and the waters of Puget Sound reflected the pastel palette as well. A row of seagulls dotted a nearby wharf. Cassie barely noticed nature's spectacular display.

"What will you do now?" she asked.

He shrugged. "I'll start over, I guess. I may have nothing—I may be broke for years—but I'll make it again someday, even if it takes the rest of my life."

"Of course you will," Cassie replied, "but you didn't have to bring me to such an expensive place to break the news to me." Even though she had ordered the cheapest item on the menu, the meal had still cost him plenty.

"I didn't bring you here for that. I just wanted you to know about it first."

"First?" she echoed.

He dug a hand into his pocket and took out a small box that made her eyes widen.

"I wanted you to know everything before I gave you this." He took a deep breath. "I love you," he said. "It would mean a lot to me if you were by my side while I struggle. Even if we have to live in a tiny apartment or a little rundown bungalow, pinching pennies and cutting corners until I make it big again, I want you with me.''

He raised the lid on the box to reveal a lovely diamond ring blazing with light. Cassie could hardly see through her tears of joy.

"Sweetheart, will you marry me?''

Overwhelmed, she threw her arms around his neck. "I love you, too," she sobbed. "And I'd be thrilled to marry you.''

She could have sworn she'd felt him stiffen with surprise.

"You would? I mean, you will?'' he stammered.

She let him go and stepped back to gaze into his face. He looked so vulnerable and confused that she had to smile through her tears.

"Yes," she repeated. "I will. Now, aren't you going to kiss your new fiancée?''

"Uh, yeah.'' With a sheepish grin, Nick bent his head. When he was done kissing her, he took the ring out of the box and slipped it onto her finger.

Holding out her hand, Cassie really looked at the diamond for the first time. It glittered like a crystal chandelier lit by a thousand candles. Trust Nick to spend money he should be using for his business on a gift for her, instead.

"It's lovely, but I don't need anything this expensive," she said. "It's how you feel that matters to me, not extraneous symbols. In the morning we can exchange this for a nice little diamond solitaire or even a cubic zirconia. You know most people can't tell they aren't the real thing. That way you can take the extra money and put it right into your business. Every little bit helps.''

For a moment, she thought he was going to get

angry. Had she gone too far and trod squarely on his masculine ego? Then his frown cleared and he pressed a kiss to the back of her hand, right next to the ring. When he lifted his head, his eyes were glowing.

"All I want is to make you happy," he murmured, and then he kissed her again.

"I should have listened to you," Nick admitted miserably as he and Bull watched the twins splashing around in a plastic wading pool behind the house. Both the kids were wearing swimsuits. Adam's trunks were covered with action heroes and Amanda was wearing the tiniest pink bikini Nick had ever seen. Cassie was in the house, putting away the laundry.

"I was dead wrong about Cassie," he continued. "It's been three weeks since I told her I could lose all my money and she hasn't bolted yet. All she does is think of ways to conserve what little of it remains."

Bull gave him a disgusted look Nick knew he fully deserved. Why hadn't he listened when Bull had tried to tell him he didn't need to test her loyalty? Since the night he'd proposed, his love for her had grown to the point where he was terrified she'd find out the truth and he'd lose her forever.

Just when he'd been about to pop the question, he'd come to the crashing realization that he couldn't ask without telling her first that he loved her. When he spoke the words he knew without a doubt that he meant them.

She'd accepted his proposal without hesitation, despite his grim description of life in a trailer. Now he regretted spoiling the moment with his silly scheme. Whenever he thought about that night he would have to remember that asking her to be his bride had been little more than a loyalty test.

"You could just tell her what you did," Bull suggested as Adam dumped a bucket of water on his sister.

"Don't pick on your sister," Nick shouted. Funny, but his feelings for the twins hadn't undergone any huge change in the past weeks. They were the same kids; he was the same man.

Amanda waved at the two men. Her cheeks were pink and her eyes glowed with happiness. What an improvement. Cassie said she hadn't had a nightmare in weeks.

When she and Nick had told the twins they were getting married, both had seemed pleased. Nick remembered how Cassie had squatted and asked them if they would be in the wedding. He'd been astounded when Adam had asked if that meant they could live with him and Cassie after they were married. Funny how kids' minds worked, he mused. There was no question of his giving up the twins; they were still his children in every way that counted.

"Well, what do you think?" Bull asked. "You gonna come clean with her? You'll feel a lot better if you do."

Bull's words brought Nick back to the present. When Nick glanced at him, he was surprised to see that Bull's face had turned a dusky red. If Nick hadn't known better, he would have thought the other man was blushing.

"I can't tell her," he said. "She'd be terribly hurt that I doubted her. All I can do is make sure she never finds out the truth."

Chapter Eleven

Except for a queasy stomach in the morning and her worries about the IRS, Cassie was living in a dream world. Nick managed to be loving and attentive despite the demands of his work and he'd even taken time off to go with her to the doctor's. If he was a little withdrawn sometimes, that was to be expected. She knew he was battling for the survival of his business, even if she didn't understand what the problems were. If only she could have been more help.

She'd called Walter several times, but all he could tell her was that the government moved slowly. Miles had been working long hours with their auditors and accountants, but he couldn't tell her much, either, except that they were painfully thorough.

"The minute I know anything for sure, I'll call you," he promised. He had seemed pleased about her engagement, smiling as he kissed her cheek and admired her ring.

The weather had been unseasonably hot the past couple of weeks. They kept the air-conditioning at the house on during the daytime, but at night they opened all the windows to the breeze that sprang up from the water.

One night Cassie woke up to see Nick coming back into the master bedroom. "Where did you go?" she asked.

"I checked on the kids."

Cassie glanced at the intercom. "I didn't hear a thing. Were they all right?"

Nick sat on the edge of the bed and took her hand. "Sleeping like little logs. The kittens didn't even stir when I went in."

Cassie cuddled back into her pillow and sighed with contentment. At least the exhaustion she'd felt the past few weeks was beginning to give way to her usual level of energy. Despite the heat she was starting to feel better.

Nick began playing with her fingers. "Do you want to go back to sleep?" he asked.

Cassie smiled up at him in the soft glow from the night-light on the dresser.

"What did you have in mind?" Their passion for each other seemed to grow with each passing day. Nick made no secret of the fact he couldn't get enough of her, and she felt the same. Now the look on his face ignited an answering hunger deep within her.

"You know that spot down by the grove of birch trees?" he asked. "It's very private, especially after dark."

Cassie's eyes widened and then she began to smile. "I imagine it would be nice and cool there on a warm night."

Nick's hand tightened on hers and his voice roughened. "Well, it's definitely worth checking out."

By the time they got to the birch grove, wearing robes and slippers and carrying an old quilt and a couple of pillows, they were giggling like teenagers. Luckily, the moon was only a quarter full, because the sky was completely cloudless. It was light enough to see their way, but if the night had been brighter, they would have stood out like convicts at a church picnic.

"This looks like a good spot," Cassie suggested. Thick moss cushioned the ground beneath her feet and a soft breeze stirred the branches overhead. "Is this what you had in mind?"

"Exactly so." Nick set down the pillows and spread out the quilt. He had suggested carrying her down here, but she'd insisted on walking. So far she'd gained only a couple of pounds. The little grove was a good distance from the house and she had told Nick she didn't want him worn out before they even arrived.

When he was done arranging the quilt, he turned her away from him so she was looking up at the stars while he held her against him.

"Isn't the sky beautiful?" he murmured.

"Yes, it is. Can you identify any of the constellations?" she asked.

"Only the Big Dipper. Science wasn't my strong point." His arms tightened. "You're the most beautiful thing I see."

Cassie turned in his arms and cupped her hand to his cheek. "I love you."

Nick lowered his head. "And I love you." He covered her mouth with his and desire rose between them, sharp and sweet. Breaking off the kiss, he helped her out of her wrap and stripped off his own robe. She was still wearing a nightgown, but he was gloriously naked and fully aroused. Her breath caught at his sheer male perfection. He hadn't taken much time for one-on-one basketball with his friend lately, but he certainly wasn't deteriorating that she could see.

Nick knelt on the quilt, pulling her gently down so she faced him. Cassie lifted her nightgown over her head and tossed it aside. There was just enough light for her to make out his expression. He watched her like a bird of prey ready to pounce. His utter concentration on her made her shiver with reaction.

Daringly, she leaned forward so her nipples brushed his chest. The cool air had puckered them into hard little buds and she shifted from side to side in a slow caress.

Nick's breath hissed in sharply. He wrapped his hands around her upper arms, anchoring her close. The kiss he gave her smoldered with promise and left her gasping. Then, before she could recover, he rolled her beneath him and covered her body with his. She'd meant to seduce; instead, she was the one burning out of control.

His hands streaked over her sensitized skin, blazing a trail his hungry mouth followed. Her fingers were buried in his hair, her teeth were clenched against a groan of pure need. As he drove her ever higher, his own breathing turned ragged. When her lips found a place to nibble and her hands grew bolder, his groan gratified her.

"I want you," he rasped. "I can't wait."

In silent invitation, she made a place for him in her deepest self. Like dancers in perfect harmony, they partnered each other, moving as two halves of the same whole. Together they sought and found intimacy in its deepest, most ultimate form.

"Not too cold?" Nick asked, drawing the quilt over Cassie's shoulders. He lay on his back and she was cuddled against him. As he looked up at the sky overhead, feeling her breath on his skin and her slight weight along his body, he'd never felt so insignificant and yet so content.

"I'm very comfortable," she murmured, dropping a kiss on his chest. When she shifted, her hair trailed across his skin like silken tassels. His hand caressed her back beneath the quilt; his other arm was propped under his head.

"How are things going at work?" she asked.

Instantly guilt flooded him, and he shifted restlessly. "Let's not talk about that." How he hated the mess he'd gotten himself into. What he needed to do was to tell her the crisis was over, but he couldn't bear to taint the memory of this night with another falsehood.

"Then why don't you tell me more about your childhood?" Cassie asked. "I'm hoping to meet your mother soon."

"We'll fly down and visit her," he promised. "She'll love you. We'll take the twins."

"That would be nice."

Her hand drifted over his stomach, causing an instant reaction. His constant hunger for her amazed him. Later, when she grew round with his child, he would have to be more careful. For now he had only to turn to her and she welcomed him with open arms and a passion that matched his own.

Struggling for control, Nick caught her hand in his. "We'd better go in," he said reluctantly. "I'd hate for the kids to wake Bull if they couldn't find us."

Cassie smothered a chuckle. "Ooh, that's an ugly picture. I guess you're right, but I hope we'll come back here again sometime."

Helping her up, Nick slipped the nightgown back over her head and put on his robe. "I have a feeling we will."

Nick had already left for work when Cassie's attorney called and asked her to come down to his office. She thought about telling Nick and then decided to wait and see if the news was good or bad. Instead, she phoned Mrs. Beagle, who promised to watch the twins for her.

"He's on the phone and then he'll be right out," Walter's secretary told Cassie when she walked into his office in downtown Seattle.

Cassie was tempted to ask Doreen if she knew what he had to say, but pumping the other woman was pointless. Cassie had been waiting for three months; a few more minutes wouldn't kill her.

Finally the door to Walter's office opened and he came out. "Sorry to keep you waiting," he said with a smile.

Cassie returned his greeting as she walked past him, her knees trembling, and sat down in a chair facing his desk. Was his expression pleased for her or edged with sympathy? She had no idea.

"I can't wait any longer," she said as he sat down behind his desk and opened a folder. "I take it you've heard something. What's the verdict?"

Walter's smile widened. "The investigation is over and they didn't find anything except for a few minor discrepancies," he replied. "I'll go over their report with you, but the bottom line is that all charges have been dropped."

Cassie stared as relief surged through her. Then sudden tears flooded her eyes.

"Oh, dear," she murmured, bowing her head.

Walter had seen her cry before. No doubt more than one client had shed tears of pain, joy or despair in this office. Now he stood and handed Cassie a tissue.

"That's okay," he soothed. "Everything is back to normal. Accounts unfrozen, assets released. And Miles would like you to call him as soon as you can. Use my phone if you'd like."

"In a minute," Cassie replied. "I'm sure he's elated, as well, but first I have to absorb this myself." She laid a protective hand on her stomach. No matter what else happened, her baby's future was assured, at least financially.

"Would you like some water?" Walter asked.

She shook her head. "No, thanks. I will use your phone, though, if you don't mind."

He circled his desk and patted her shoulder lightly. "Go right ahead. I'll give you some privacy."

Before he left, she remembered to thank him and then she reached for the receiver.

* * *

Miles had insisted on treating her to lunch to celebrate. Cassie had checked in with Mrs. Beagle and she could hardly wait to give Nick the news, but she wanted to tell him in person. Sympathetic to his own ongoing crisis, she didn't think it would be appropriate to burst in on him at work with her happy news, so she resigned herself to waiting until he got home that evening.

Meanwhile, she and Miles were just finishing lunch.

"There's no way I can thank you for all you've done to save the company," she told him as she pushed aside the remains of her crab salad. "If there's anything I can do, please let me know." Robert had left the business to them jointly, but Miles was the one who knew it inside out.

The waiter took their empty plates and served their dessert and coffee, while Cassie glanced around the busy room. In the running of the company, she planned to stay very much in the background and let Miles take charge. Even though she trusted him implicitly, she would never be as naive as she had with Robert himself. As soon as she had the time, she wanted to begin learning more about their holdings so she could at least be informed.

"There is one thing we need to discuss," Miles replied, ignoring his amaretto mousse and leaning his elbows on the table.

Cassie took a bite of kiwi sorbet and listened attentively as he described the subdivision he wanted to sell and outlined his reasons.

"Dad bought it when he thought diversifying was a good idea," he explained. "Now that I'm running things, I want to concentrate on our areas of strength.

I've had a good offer for this division and I'd like to take it. The proceeds from a sale this large will enable us to buy back a big block of our own stock.''

"Why do that?" Cassie asked.

"It's the kind of gesture that shows faith in our financial solidity and it should go a long way in squelching any lingering rumors that we're in trouble.''

"I understand," she replied. In theory, at least, what he was saying made sense. "I'll support whatever you think is for the best."

Miles leaned back in his chair. "I'd be happy to go over the paperwork with you before you sign anything.''

"I'd appreciate that." She had mentioned to him before that she wanted to understand what he was doing, even though she had no intention of interfering with his management of the company. Not that she could if she had wanted to. Her powers were limited and that was why she appreciated Miles's taking the time to consult her.

"I'm surprised Nick hasn't already mentioned the possible buyout to you," Miles commented as he dug into his mousse.

Nick? Cassie's spoon froze halfway to her mouth. "I beg your pardon?"

"It's one of his companies that made the offer. I assumed he might have discussed it with you already." Miles's eyes twinkled. "Or don't you talk about business?" he asked teasingly.

Now Cassie recalled how carefully Nick had questioned her about her involvement with RWC. At the time she had assumed he was merely curious. An uneasy feeling slithered down her spine. Carefully, she set down her spoon.

"Just how much is this deal going to cost him?" she asked her stepson.

When Miles named the figure, her eyes widened. "My goodness, but that's a lot of money."

"Well, it isn't all cash," Miles explained. "It's more complicated than that. But, yes, it is a relatively big deal. Obviously, Nick's company is in excellent shape financially to contemplate this kind of expansion."

Miles's words confirmed the suspicion that had started to churn like acid in Cassie's stomach.

"His company is solvent?" she asked. "There's no chance he's facing financial ruin?"

Miles frowned. "Not unless he's bluffing with this offer, and I can't see why he would. He came to me with it—I didn't solicit him."

Cassie gripped the edge of the table to keep her hands from trembling. "You're sure?"

"Absolutely. Word is out that Nick's company just closed a huge deal with a Hong Kong investment group that was highly profitable to him. I can't imagine that things could have turned around so quickly. Why do you ask?"

Sick with dread, Cassie struggled for a reply that would calm Miles's concerns. "I guess I really misunderstood something he was telling me," she said, ad-libbing as she went. "He was talking about some other company and I thought he'd changed the subject to Kincaid Corp." She managed an embarrassed smile. "I wasn't paying close attention. I guess I'd better ask him again."

Miles finished his dessert and reached for the

check. "That's a pretty big mix-up," he chided her gently. "You wouldn't want to start a false rumor now, would you?"

When Cassie pulled up in front of the building that housed Nick's company, she shut off the motor and stared blankly into space. The question that kept circling her brain like a plane searching for a place to land was *why?* Why had Nick lied to her? Why had he pretended to be in danger of going broke? She hadn't misunderstood; he'd told her several times he might lose everything.

Deliberately, Cassie pressed her fingers to her throbbing temples and tried to sort out the chaotic thoughts crashing through her head. She had been so worried about losing everything. Had he somehow been trying to make her feel better by letting her think he was going through the same thing?

No, that didn't make sense. She'd only been more worried that neither of them would have any money.

Money. It all came back to that. She'd taken the nanny position because she needed the money. What if he'd lost his and couldn't pay her?

What would she have done? Quit? Abandoned him and the twins? Was *that* what he expected? No, she loved him. She wouldn't have left just because—

Suddenly Cassie sat up straighter. Had he been *testing* her? Was *that* what he thought she was after—his money? She shook her head in violent denial and then she noticed a passerby staring curiously. Cassie turned her head away.

Nick wouldn't do that to her.

The longer Cassie went over Nick's story and what Miles had told her today, the more obvious was the conclusion. The facts were undeniable. Nick was afraid she was interested in him for his money, or financial security, or whatever. He'd even believed, at least temporarily, that she was willing to pass off another man's baby in her attempt to land *him*. What Cassie had been so willing to forgive as a temporary lapse in judgment had been only a small part of the man's massive paranoia, of his gigantic ego.

Slapping her hands against the steering wheel until her palms stung, she was torn between desperate hurt and raging fury. She barely resisted banging her head against the wheel.

How could she have been so colossally stupid to fall for another corporate type with a computer where his heart should have been, the morals of a scam artist, the principles of a junk-bond salesman and a handful of microchips instead of a brain?

The engagement ring he'd given her caught the light and winked at her mockingly. As she stared down at it, the ring seemed to grow tighter, heavier, weighing down her entire hand. Furious, Cassie yanked it off and tossed it into the glove compartment. Then her common sense reared its head and she locked the compartment carefully.

She was barely aware of the angry tears streaming down her face until one dribbled into her mouth. Blotting the moisture with a tissue from her purse, Cassie gritted her teeth. She would not, *would not*, cry in front of Nick. She wasn't crushed by his duplicity; she was mad as hell!

Impatiently, she waited for her eyes to clear, and then with hands that shook, she repaired her makeup before she left the car and went into his building. Some of what she was feeling must have shown on her face. Several people looked at her and then looked quickly away. The guard in the lobby gave her a hard stare, but he didn't attempt to stop her from marching toward the bank of elevators and slapping her hand against the button.

When Cassie got off at Nick's floor and crossed the expanse of plush carpet, his secretary, Opal, greeted her with a pleasant smile. They had met when Cassie stopped by the office with the twins.

"Is he expecting you?" Opal asked.

Cassie shook her head and dredged up a smile in return. "It's a surprise."

Opal's hand hesitated on its way to the intercom button.

"In that case, why don't you go right in," she suggested with a knowing look. "He's alone and I'm sure it would be all right."

Fleetingly, Cassie hoped the other woman didn't lose her job over this. Then she forgot about Opal as she turned the knob and pushed open the door to Nick's office.

He was seated behind his desk. When he glanced up and saw her, his expression of surprise changed immediately to one of welcome.

"Hi, honey."

As Cassie shut the door behind her, he came around to her, arms outstretched.

She endured his kiss of greeting, afraid her heart would break. Had it all been a lie?—the proposal, the declaration of love? Had any of it been real?

As Nick finally let her go, she dismissed the litany of questions, afraid they'd make her cry those tears she'd vowed not to shed in his presence.

Blissfully ignorant of the emotions churning inside

her, Nick grabbed her hands in his and gave her a
smile that oozed with charm. Damn, but he was still
handsome, still overwhelmingly appealing to her.
Why didn't his duplicity repulse her? How long
would it take for the love she felt to die?

What right had he to test her the way he had?
Cassie recalled how she'd agonized over his situation
and her own inability to help, not because the money
was important to her, but because she knew the company was important to him. He'd built it from nothing.

Her rage came back in a gigantic rush.

"What happened to your ring?" Nick asked, staring down at her bare hand. "You didn't lose it, did
you?"

"Maybe I pawned it," she suggested airily, flut-
tering her lashes at him. Gritting her teeth, she remembered how she had offered to exchange it for a
cheaper one when he'd first presented it to her. Good
Lord, she'd felt guilty that he'd spent so much of his
precious money on her.

He'd refused to listen at the time and she had been
so afraid she'd somehow wounded his precious male
ego. No doubt it had been his conscience giving him
fits. If he even had a conscience. Right now she seriously doubted that he did.

At her flippant reply, he gaped at her, red climbing
up his neck to spill across his cheeks.

"You're kidding, aren't you?"

Was that guilt coloring his face?

Pulling her hands free of his grip, Cassie walked
to the window that overlooked downtown Bellevue.
She took a deep breath and spun around.

"Could I use the money to buy into the great deal

you're setting up with RWC?'' she asked. ''Miles tells me what you're paying will enable our company to buy back a huge block of stock and inspire confidence in our financial strength.''

Nick opened his mouth, but nothing came out. After a moment he raked a hand over his face. ''Damn,'' he muttered, head bowed. His gaze met hers, and he pleaded for understanding. ''I'm sorry. I'd hoped you wouldn't find out.''

''Aren't you even going to bother trying to deny it?'' she asked, her voice rising.

He looked away, shaking his head. ''No. I'm too ashamed.''

His bald admission shocked her, but it wasn't enough to stem the sense of betrayal that drove her. ''You should be.''

He took a couple of steps in her direction, but she backed quickly away. Stopping, he lifted one hand in a beseeching gesture. ''Let me explain.''

''Explain what?'' she demanded. ''That you thought I was a round-heeled little gold digger looking for a new sugar daddy? That you figured I'd married for money once and I'd do it again? That you didn't trust in my love or your own judgment?''

Now she was the one stalking him. She stepped closer until she was glaring up into his face. He'd gone pale and she could see each individual lash that framed his gray eyes, each hair that was combed back from his broad forehead.

''I didn't think that.''

''Oh, please!'' Deliberately, she lowered her voice. ''Did you ever love me?'' The question was torn from her before she even knew she was going to ask it.

His eyes darkened with some emotion she couldn't identify.

"Yes," he groaned, reaching for her. "I did. I do. Always. And I'm so sorry I hurt you."

Before he could touch her, Cassie eluded him.

"You asked me if the baby was yours," she whispered with a protective hand on her stomach. "You wanted proof. I let that go, so you had to do this? What was next, I wonder?"

Nick closed his eyes and shook his head. "We'll forget all about the paternity test," he offered. "Just say you'll forgive me."

It was Cassie's turn to shake her head emphatically. "No," she said quietly. "This whole relationship was a lie, a *test*. What would you have done if I'd failed? Would you have thrown me out in the street?"

"Of course not!" He looked confused. "We need to talk, but not when you're so upset. It's bad for the baby."

Cassie raised a warning finger and shook it at him. "Don't you dare use this baby as an excuse."

He made an uncharacteristically indecisive gesture. "I'm sorry. I don't know what I was thinking." His mouth took on a bitter twist. "My father abandoned my mother when she was pregnant with me. I would never have done that to you. You have to believe me."

"Sure, if I'd passed your test!" Cassie shot back at him. She couldn't allow pity for his childhood to influence her. He was a grown man; he should have known better.

"You could have trusted me," she said, giving him a long look.

When he didn't say anything, she stepped around him and headed for the door.

"Cassie," he called as she yanked it open, "We'll talk again later, okay?"

She didn't bother to reply.

After Cassie left, Nick dropped into his chair as if his legs had been shot out from under him. His worst nightmare had come to pass, just as Bull had warned that it would.

Bitterly, he buried his face in his hands. Opal buzzed him, but he ignored her. A minute later, there was a knock on his door. When he still didn't respond, the door was quietly shut tight. He knew Opal would let no one disturb him until he told her to.

Nick's first impulse was to follow Cassie back to his house and to keep at her until she forgave him. He'd never been one to jump at his first impulse.

He'd done everything but lie down and beg her to walk on him, he told himself. He'd admitted his mistake, he'd apologized and he'd tried to make amends. What more could he do? What did she expect—that he prostrate himself before her and offer to do penance?

The more Nick went over the last scene in his office, the more self-righteous he felt. He'd been correct not to chase after her. She needed time to think about the situation, to reconsider. Sure, he was responsible for a grave error in judgment, but she had to look at his side. There were some sound reasons for him to feel the way he had. The precedent, so to speak, had been set.

Cassie must understand why he'd be especially cautious, since he'd been duped before. And her situation, from the outside, appeared at least to have the possibility of being suspicious.

No, he realized, that wasn't an argument he'd be wise to pursue. She had married an older, wealthy man, but if she claimed to have loved him at the time, Nick had no choice but to believe her.

Now that he knew Cassie better, he had no problem with that. He'd been an idiot; that he freely admitted. And he'd tell her tonight—if she was willing to listen.

One of the hardest things he'd have to do was to face Bull. Wouldn't his housekeeper just gloat when he found out that exactly what he'd warned Nick about had come to pass?

No, Nick realized with a sigh; Bull wouldn't gloat. He wasn't the kind of person to enjoy someone else's unhappiness. But he sure as hell would point out that he'd been right in warning Nick to tell Cassie the truth before she heard it somewhere else. That much, at least, Bull wouldn't be able to resist.

An hour later Nick was doing his best to concentrate on a report from one of his midlevel managers, when Opal buzzed him. When he hadn't made an appearance after Cassie left, Opal had finally brought him a cup of coffee. He suspected her real intent had been to assess damages.

Since then, she'd been heading off his phone calls, but now her voice came over the intercom with her usual calm efficiency.

"There's a call for you on two."

"Who is it?" Nick asked.

"Mr. Wylie. He says it's urgent."

Bull wouldn't call him at work unless something

had happened to one of the twins. His heart in his throat, Nick picked up the receiver.

"It's Cassie," Bull said without preamble. "You'd better get here as fast as you can."

Dear Lord, Nick thought as he leaped to his feet, she must be losing the baby.

Chapter Twelve

When Cassie slipped into the house, she could hear Bull slamming around in the kitchen. She had waited to come by until she could be reasonably sure the twins would be taking their naps and Mrs. Beagle would be dozing, as well.

Feeling like a burglar, Cassie crept upstairs. The door to the twins' room was partially closed and all was quiet. She went into her own bedroom and shut the door behind her. With a little luck, she could do what she had to and be out of there without anyone being the wiser.

She packed all her belongings and then she tiptoed across the hall. Amanda was awake. When she saw Cassie, she sat up in bed.

Cassie pressed a warning finger to her lips. Adam's eyes were shut, his breathing steady, but the adjoining door was partway open. From the other room, Cassie could hear Mrs. Beagle snoring softly.

"Why are you here?" Amanda whispered.

"I had to get something," Cassie whispered back. She glanced uneasily at Adam, but he didn't stir. She'd hoped to bid them a silent goodbye while they both slept. Instead, she gave Amanda a kiss on the cheek. "Have a good nap," Cassie told her.

"When are you coming home?" Amanda asked.

The innocent question made Cassie's heart ache. She couldn't admit the truth. "Later," she said vaguely. "Go to sleep." With fingers that trembled, she bent over Adam and pushed his hair off his warm forehead. He stirred and muttered something in his sleep.

Cassie gave Amanda one last wave. After waving back, she obediently lay back down and shut her eyes.

As Cassie ducked into her room again for the bags she'd left by the bed, she felt the prickle of tears. Blinking them away, she crept back downstairs to find Bull standing guard by the front door, a feather duster in one hand.

"Looks like you're really leaving this time," he said, flicking the duster over a framed pen-and-ink drawing of the waterfront.

"How did you know?" Cassie bluffed.

He glanced pointedly at the bag she carried. "I saw that in your room." He gave the vase sitting on a side table a swipe with the duster. "Have you told the kids that you're going?"

Cassie bit her lip to stop its trembling. "No. I couldn't."

"They'll be upset." He stuck the feather duster in

the back pocket of his jeans. "It's a warm day. How about a glass of iced tea before you take off?"

"I'm sorry," she replied. "Not this time." She'd miss him, she realized. In his own gruff way, he'd been a friend to her. At least she felt more confident leaving the twins partly in his care than she would have a few weeks ago, before he'd discovered that children were people, too.

"Can't you and the boss work this out?" Bull asked, sidling around until he stood between Cassie and the door.

She ignored his question. Instead, she asked, "Did you know he told me he was facing bankruptcy?"

The expression on the housekeeper's face was all the answer she needed. She tried to step around him and he shifted his massive bulk so he was still blocking her exit.

"I told him it was a bad idea. How'd you find out?"

"My stepson told me. Nick's company is buying one of our subdivisions."

"How will you manage?" Bull asked. He knew her assets had been frozen.

Cassie's smile was edged with bitterness. "The investigation is over. RWC has been cleared."

Bull fidgeted with his earring. "That's good news, at least. Does Nick know?"

Cassie was getting restless. She needed to be on her way. "I didn't tell him. I had more pressing business on my mind."

Bull's eyebrows went up. "You talked to Nick?"

"I went to his office to confront him."

"What did he say?" Bull asked.

Cassie began to suspect he was stalling. Had he

called Nick? The last thing she wanted was another confrontation, especially in front of the children. "He offered to waive the paternity test," she said bitterly. "I don't know how I resisted. Now I have to go."

Bull muttered something. Cassie didn't quite hear what Bull muttered, but she did catch "stupid" and "jackass." While he was distracted, she darted around him and grabbed the doorknob.

"Thanks for everything," she said, standing on tiptoe to kiss his bristly cheek. "Take care of the kids."

Before Bull could reply, before she could start to cry again, Cassie fled.

"Where is she?" Nick saw Bull as soon as he rushed in the front door and crossed the entry. Through the open kitchen window he could hear the twins in the backyard. Mrs. Beagle's car was still in the driveway, but Cassie's wasn't.

"Gone." Bull looked disgusted. "I stalled her as long as I could."

"I got stuck in road construction. Where did she go? What did she say? Is she all right?" Nick asked. "Is the baby okay?"

"As far as I know." Bull wiped his hands on a towel and tossed it to the counter. "I told you she'd find out and you'd be sorry."

Nick was in no mood for I-told-you-sos. He gave Bull a black look and ran up the stairs. In Cassie's room, he searched for some evidence that she hadn't fled for good, but everything she'd left here when she'd moved to the master suite with him was gone. Even her bathroom was empty.

Swearing under his breath, he went down the hall

to his own room. The extra clothes she'd hung in his closet were missing and so was the nightgown she kept folded under the pillow. Only the scent of her cologne lingered to torment him.

Nick sat down on the bed and buried his face in the pillow as the full realization of the situation hit him. Because of his own lack of trust he'd lost her, perhaps for good this time.

"Well, Mama, I wish you could tell me what to do now," Cassie said as she sat with Adele Hansen.

Cassie's mother continued to stare out the window, picking restlessly with her fingers at the afghan covering her knees. Her gaze darted to Cassie and then back to the ducks in the pond outside. "Where's my lunch?" she asked querulously. "My daughter's visiting today and I want my lunch before she gets here."

"Mama, I'm here," Cassie said patiently. At least she didn't have to worry anymore about how to pay the nursing home bill.

Would her mother notice when Cassie began to show? Her stomach was still flat, but that situation was bound to change. At least the nausea had passed.

"I'm going to have a baby," Cassie blurted, and then her shoulders sagged. What was the point?

"You always wanted a child," Adele commented in a dreamy voice without turning from the window.

Cassie held her breath, but nothing else was said. After a few moments, she got up and put her hand on her mother's shoulder. "You're finally going to be a grandmother," she said softly.

"My daughter's coming today," Adele repeated. "I want my lunch now."

* * *

"Cassie told me she'd be back," Amanda insisted. "When is she coming? I miss her already."

"Me, too," Adam chimed in as Nick tried to find his son's other sneaker. "We want Cassie."

Amanda joined in the chant and their voices rose in unison, "We want Cassie—we want Cassie."

No kidding, Nick thought with a fresh stab of pain. I want her, too.

"Do you remember when you last saw your shoe?" he shouted above their escalating voices as he got down on his hands and knees.

Adam's nose was runny and his temperature was a little high; Amanda had a cough Nick didn't like the sound of and she'd been awake in the night with an earache. Both children were scheduled for visits to the doctor today and Nick hadn't found a permanent replacement yet for Cassie, so he was taking them in himself before he went to work.

Bending, he spotted Adam's missing sneaker in the far corner under the bed. He also found two Oreo cookies, a picture book and three toy mice that belonged to the kittens.

"No more food in the bedroom," he stated, holding up the cookies.

"Cassie let us," Amanda replied stubbornly.

Nick sent her a stern glance and she lapsed into silence, her lower lip jutting out.

"Why can't Cassie take us to the doctor?" Adam asked as Nick wiped his nose with a tissue.

"Because Cassie isn't here." Nick's patience was beginning to run thin as he helped Adam with his socks and shoes.

"Why don't you tell her to come back?"

Adam began waving one stockinged foot in wide circles. When Nick chased it with the shoe, he giggled. Finally Nick grabbed his ankle.

"Cassie doesn't want to come back right now." In the three weeks since she'd left, he had called her house a dozen times. Her dragon of a housekeeper made Bull seem like a steer in comparison. Not once had Nick managed to get past the woman. Not once had she given him a drop of information. She was about as flexible as a brick wall.

He'd driven to Cassie's house on several occasions. He'd taken flowers, candy, had even tried to bribe the housekeeper with a hundred-dollar bill. That time she shut the door in his face.

Even Max had growled at him on the one occasion Nick was able to get a glimpse of the dog. Cassie he hadn't seen at all. Perhaps her car had been in the garage.

Nick had thought she'd crack before now. He was nearly ready to set up camp in front of her house until she agreed to see him. Only the whimpering remnants of his pride had kept him from doing so.

He wasn't about to share any of this information with his children. One thing he had done was to contact an attorney to find out if Janine would relinquish her parental rights to the twins. He wanted no problems later on if her maternal instincts suddenly came to life, or if their biological father appeared.

According to Bull, calling the attorney was the one thing Nick had done right since Cassie had first told him she was pregnant.

"Is Cassie mad at you?" Amanda asked.

Nick was trying to tame her curly hair with a brush. It had grown enough that it stuck out in a dozen directions. He had no idea what to do about it. Adam's blond locks were getting shaggy, too. Perhaps Nick would take them both to his barber this weekend.

"Yeah, Cassie's mad at me," he admitted as Amanda looked in her mirror and frowned.

"Why don't you just tell her you're sorry?" Adam suggested with adult wisdom. "Then she won't be mad and she'll come back to us."

He grinned up at Nick as if to say, *why didn't you think of that?*

"Sometimes things are more complicated for grown-ups," Nick replied as he sat Amanda in his lap and helped with her shoes and socks. She wore sandals with Velcro fasteners, so she could do them up herself.

"I just wish she'd come back," Adam grumbled. "I miss her way more than I missed Mom before."

His words sent a chill through Nick. So did he.

By the time he had taken them to the pediatrician, endured the waiting room full of other children coughing, sneezing and crying, tried to remember the doctor's instructions and brought them home two hours later with several pamphlets and four separate prescriptions, *he* wished she would come back, too, and not just because he ached from missing her. From a practical standpoint, if she were here, then *she* would be the one taking them to the pediatrician and administering their medicine.

"Perhaps you should give the poor man a break," Emma said over fresh-squeezed lemonade and the sugar cookies she'd baked that morning.

"Why's that?" Cassie asked. "Because he trusted

me? Because he always told the truth? Because he accepted this baby with as much joy as I did?'' She was tired of Nick, tired of thinking about him, tired of missing him, tired of talking about him to Emma and, especially, tired of hearing about how she was being too hard on him.

''Because, misguided as he's been, I'd bet my best marble rolling pin the man loves you,'' Emma said, sipping her lemonade.

Cassie made a rude noise. ''And what led you to that conclusion?''

Emma's eyes sparkled behind her glasses. ''Because he's had to put up with me for the past three weeks and yet he's still calling.''

''But not as often.'' Despite her depression, Cassie had to chuckle. ''You're such a dragon, too.''

''I can be,'' Emma replied. ''Did I tell you he offered me a bribe?''

''Only a hundred dollars.'' Cassie's voice was scornful. ''You should be insulted that he put such a small price on your loyalty.''

''Perhaps he would have upped the offer if I hadn't slammed the door in his face.''

Cassie bit into a cookie. Much more sitting around doing nothing but indulging her sweet tooth and she'd have a *real* problem—none of the new, looser clothes she'd bought would fit.

How much longer would Nick persist? she wondered. How much longer would she wake up in the night, cheeks wet with tears, throat raw with wanting, before she began getting over him? And how would she ever be able to look at the child of their love and keep her heart from breaking all over again?

''So,'' Emma began, snapping a cookie in two and

slipping half of it to Max while Cassie pretended not to notice, "are you going to forgive him?"

"No." Cassie willed her resolution to remain strong. "I forgave him for the way he acted when I told him I was pregnant because I thought he had a good reason for it. I don't care how good a reason he had for pretending he was losing his money. It just doesn't matter anymore."

Finishing her lemonade while Emma gave her a sympathetic look, Cassie wished with all her heart that what she'd said were even remotely true. The real truth was she suspected she was going to love Nicolas Kincaid for as long as she lived. Forgiving him, though, was something else entirely.

"Mrs. Hansen, I'm a friend of your daughter's," Nick said to the frail woman staring out the window. He could see that her hair was a darker blond than Cassie's, heavily mixed with gray and cut in a short bob.

Cassie had told him her mother had good days. He could only pray this was one of them, since he was running out of options.

The woman turned and looked at Nick with eyes only a little paler that her daughter's. Her forehead pleated into a puzzled frown and his heart sank.

"Are you Nick?" she asked.

"Yes!" In his excitement, he grabbed her hand and gave it a firm squeeze.

She smiled and patted her hair with her free hand. "It's nice to meet you at last."

"You, too, Mrs. Hansen. Cassie talks about you all the time."

"Please, call me 'Adele.'" She hesitated. "I'm

afraid my memory isn't what it used to be, so forgive me if I seem a little vague. How is Cassie?'' She glanced past him as if she expected to see her daughter appear.

"Cassie's not with me today," he said. "The truth is that she and I had an argument and I don't know where she's gone. I thought you might be able to help me out."

Adele pressed her lips together and studied him. "If you don't mind my asking, what was the argument about?"

Nick debated just how much to tell her, but he had a feeling she wouldn't help him if she suspected he wasn't being entirely truthful. Shifting in his chair, he tried to figure out the best place to start.

"I'm a fairly successful man," he began haltingly.

Adele tipped her head to the side as she eyed him. "My son-in-law had a lot of money, too," she remarked. "I didn't care for him much. Money doesn't guarantee happiness."

Nick couldn't argue with her there. "I'm afraid that in the beginning, I wondered if it might be my money that attracted Cassie."

The frown came back. "Robert left my daughter well-fixed."

Briefly, Nick explained about the IRS investigation. "Everything is straightened out now," he concluded. Bull had enlightened him. "But for a while things looked a little dicey."

"The poor child!" Adele exclaimed. "She must have been frantic. This place isn't cheap. I imagine that's why she went to work for you in the first place, isn't it? She didn't explain how you two met, at least not that I remember."

He admitted that it had been why Cassie had taken the position as a nanny. Then he explained about Janine and the twins, omitting only what he'd discovered at the hospital.

"Under the circumstances, can you understand why I let my doubts get in the way of my feelings for your daughter?"

"I can see why trust might have been an issue with you. What did you do that made Cassie angry?" she asked.

As Nick described the test he'd devised, he realized once again how stupid he'd been to risk her love for his own foolish pride. He'd be happy to give Cassie *all* his money just to get her back.

"I know she was hurt, but I thought she'd cool off eventually and we could talk things out. Only, now she's disappeared and that housekeeper of hers won't tell me where she's gone."

Adele leaned forward and patted his hand. "You really love my girl, don't you?"

He nodded, swallowing the knot of longing that threatened to stick in his throat. "She means everything to me." What if he'd lost her for good?

"You know she's pregnant?" Adele asked.

The abrupt question startled him. "She told you?"

Now Adele hesitated, her gaze shifting away and then back again. "I think so." She rubbed a hand across her forehead and then she raised pleading eyes to Nick. "Am I remembering right? She is expecting, isn't she?"

"Yes, we're having a baby. That's another reason I'm concerned for her."

Adele seemed satisfied with his reply, but she said,

"I'm sorry I can't help you, but I have no idea where she's gone."

Nick tried not to let his disappointment show, as he got to his feet. He didn't want to risk upsetting the older woman any further. "You've been very kind," he said as he bent and squeezed her hand. "Is there anything you need? Anything I can get for you?"

Slowly, Adele shook her head. It was obvious she was trying hard to concentrate.

"Talk to her boy," she said, frowning. "He might know where she's gone."

"Her boy?" Nick echoed, puzzled. "I don't know who you mean."

Adele licked her lips. "I can't think of his name. The older boy."

Nick had a sudden inspiration. "You mean Miles Kincaid, her stepson?"

Adele's expression cleared immediately. "Yes, that's the one. Talk to Miles. And come back to see me again sometime soon."

"You look exhausted," Miles told Cassie when he met her for an early supper at a small fish-and-chips place near Juanita Beach.

"I haven't been sleeping well." She knew she needed rest for the baby's sake, but she spent her nights tossing and turning, alternating between missing Nick and bitterly resenting him. Worried he would find a way to confront her, she had moved to Miles's beach house a couple of days before.

"I've learned some things about your Mr. Kincaid," Miles said as soon as they'd ordered and sat down at one of the small tables.

"I don't think I want to know," Cassie replied.

"What has he told you about his background?" Miles asked, ignoring her comment.

"He told me once his mother raised him. He didn't mention his father and I didn't ask. Why?"

"His father was Morris Blackwell."

"The banker?" Cassie asked.

"Banking and then some," Miles replied. "He was the leading local financier of his time, owned television stations, a mortgage company and had his fingers in numerous other pies as well as the biggest savings and loan in the state."

"My goodness," Cassie exclaimed.

"According to my sources, Blackwell didn't acknowledge Nick or even meet him, although the resemblance between them was plain to see. Nick's mother never married and no one seems to know if Blackwell ever gave her or Nick any money, but I'm guessing he didn't. The man wasn't exactly known as a philanthropist and no claim was made against his estate, either."

"Nick's a very proud man," Cassie remarked. "That background might explain his nervousness around the twins when I first met him," she mused as she pleated the fabric of her sundress with her fingers. "He almost seemed afraid of them."

"He never had a father's influence," Miles replied. "Was he coming around before you left?"

Cassie felt a burst of pride that she had to struggle to subdue. "The improvement was amazing." She told Miles about the kittens, the trip to the zoo and the time she'd walked in on Nick playing toy cars on the floor with Adam, complete with engine sounds.

Miles steepled his fingers and propped up his chin. "Sounds like a man who can learn," he remarked. "Are you sure you can't forgive him?"

Cassie's voice rose. "I don't know!" The only other patron in the café and the cook both looked up. Embarrassed, she modified her voice. "That's what's so difficult. I'm not sure he even understood why what he did was so despicable."

Quickly she told Miles about Nick's reaction to the news about her pregnancy.

"Why did you stay with him after that?" Miles demanded.

Cassie made a vague gesture with her hand. "There were extenuating circumstances. He'd just gotten some very personal news that no doubt influenced his reaction to my announcement. At the time, I chose to forgive him."

"And now?"

Clearly, Miles didn't understand.

She shook her head slowly. "Now I don't know what to do."

"Well, take your time," he advised her. "Stay at the beach house as long as you want. No need to rush into anything."

Cassie patted her stomach. "No reason except for this little guy or girl. But you're right. I have close to six months to make up my mind before I need to deal with junior here." Not that Nick would necessarily still be around then.

Miles pushed back his chair. "I'm not trying to tell you what to do," he said. "I just want you to be happy. Both of you."

Cassie patted his hand where it lay on the table.

"I know. Thanks for everything. Now, I'd better let you go."

Miles walked her to her car. Glancing pointedly at her stomach, he said, "Be sure to keep me posted. I worry about you both."

Nick had met Miles briefly when they'd first discussed the deal between Kincaid Corporation and RWC, but Nick hadn't been involved directly in the subsequent meetings. Still, he wasn't surprised when Miles agreed to see him without an appointment.

He was surprised at Miles's opening salvo.

"If you're here about Cassie, there's nothing I can tell you," he said as soon as Nick had entered his office. He stood in front of his desk, his feet braced and his hands clasped behind his back.

Nick studied him with interest, trying without success to see some resemblance to Cassie's late husband. Miles might have his father's coloring and even his intelligence, but the single-minded, go-for-the-throat ambition Robert was known for seemed to be missing. Instead, Miles was already gaining a reputation in financial circles for innovative employee benefits and philanthropic gestures.

"I don't know what Cassie told you—" Nick began.

"She told me everything." Miles perched on the corner of his desk and pointed negligently to a chair. "This visit is probably a waste of time for both of us."

"She told you about our argument?" Nick asked.

"You mean the little falsehood about your probable bankruptcy?" Miles's voice was edged with scorn. "I'm not sorry to admit I was the one who shot that story out of the water."

Nick gritted his teeth. No doubt he had it coming.

"Did she tell you about the baby?"

Now Miles's expression was openly hostile. "I'd say you were the one who needed a paternity test, just to see if you'd be a fit parent. Cassie did admit to noticing some improvement in the way you treat your other children, though."

Nick half rose from the chair, ignoring Miles's dig. "You've seen her?"

Miles nodded.

"How is she?" Nick demanded. "Is she taking care of herself?"

"This hasn't been easy on her, but basically she's fine."

Nick breathed a sigh of relief and sat back down.

"No thanks to you," Miles added.

Nick's grin was derisive; he just wasn't sure who it was aimed at, Miles or himself.

"You're probably right. I don't suppose you'd believe me if I told you I've learned the error of my ways?"

He thought he saw a gleam of curiosity in Miles's gaze. The other man stuffed his hands into his pockets.

"Convince me," he said as he turned toward the bank of windows.

Nick stared at his back and struggled with the urge to tell him he didn't follow orders from an arrogant pup. Then he reconsidered and took a moment to organize his thoughts while Miles watched the activity outside the office window. It was damn difficult speaking to his back—a ploy Nick himself had used more than once in business dealings.

Deliberately, he waited until Miles finally faced him again.

"I want to know where Cassie is," Nick said. "She wouldn't have gone anywhere without letting you know how to get in touch with her. If you refuse to tell me where she is, I'll rescind my offer to buy that division you want to unload and I'll make sure no one else wants it, either." He stared at Miles, narrow eyed.

Miles raised an eyebrow. "How will threatening me help your cause?"

It was Nick's turn to look away. He raked a hand through his hair. "I need to see for myself that she's all right," he admitted hoarsely. "And I have to talk to her."

"If you were to find her," Miles asked, "what would you say?"

"That's personal." Nick still had a little pride left. He might be prepared to toss it in the dirt at Cassie's feet, but that didn't mean he was going to prostrate himself before her stepson, as well.

Miles shrugged. "She's been badly hurt. What guarantee do I have that you won't hurt her again?"

Nick debated rapidly. He was out of options. Without Miles's cooperation, there was no telling when he might finally succeed in tracking her down? With a last reluctant sigh, he began talking.

When he was finally through, Miles looked at him thoughtfully.

"Sorry about that paternity test crack." His voice was gruff.

"Will you tell me where she is?" Nick demanded.

"I told her I wouldn't."

Miles rocked back on his heels as Nick waited impatiently, wondering if Bull and a tire iron would ensure Miles's cooperation. Probably not.

"What you need," Miles suggested finally, "is a nice quiet visit to my beach house in Juanita. You could unwind, think about things, ponder your mistakes."

Nick stared as if Miles had lost his mind. "I don't have time for that."

Miles held up a detaining hand. "You should make time. The beach house is getting a reputation as a good place to hide out and think. Take the twins with you. They might enjoy it, too." He straightened and circled the desk. "Here, why don't I write down the address and some directions for you?"

Chapter Thirteen

As Cassie sat in an old rocking chair on the porch of the beach house, she realized that solitude was beginning to weigh heavily on her. Since her dinner with Miles a couple of days ago, Max had been her only companion. He was a great dog, but his vocabulary was definitely limited. She missed the twins; she missed Bull and the kittens. Most of all, despite her best efforts at eradicating her feelings, she missed Nick.

Just this morning after stepping out of the shower, she'd studied the shape of her tummy in the mirror. Was it slightly rounder than it had been the day before? How much longer until she looked pregnant? She could hardly wait to see the evidence of her fertility.

Meanwhile, she was eating carefully and taking the prenatal vitamins her doctor had prescribed. She walked on the beach, did crossword puzzles, got caught up on her reading and still spent too much time thinking about Nick and what had gone wrong.

Had there been more she could have done to reassure him? Had she acted too hastily in leaving when she did? Should she have taken his phone calls? The questions plagued her relentlessly.

Despite what he'd done, she knew that basically he was a good, caring man. The twins had turned his life upside down, but he'd learned to cope—even to thrive as a father.

Cassie wondered what would happen to Adam and Mandy now. Did Nick intend to keep them? More questions.

At some point, she would have to face him, if only to find out what he intended to do about this child. As it did whenever she thought of her baby, her hand went protectively to her stomach. Under the circumstances, would he insist on a paternity test, or had he meant what he said when he'd offered to forgo it?

Cassie glanced at her watch. In a little while, she would go inside, fix herself a salad, maybe have a nap. Tomorrow or the next day, she'd think about going home. Meanwhile, all she had to do was to sit here and try not to think about the man whom, in spite of herself, she still loved and missed with every fiber of her being.

Cassie's stomach growled. She was thinking about going in, when she heard children's laughter from down the shoreline. Beside her, Max got to his feet, tail wagging. He ran down the steps, looked back at Cassie and whined anxiously.

"What is it, boy? Sounds just like the twins, doesn't it?" she asked.

Max whined again and began to dance with excitement.

Cassie got to her feet and shielded her gaze with her hand. Max loved to run on the beach, but she didn't want some stranger to have a heart attack when he saw the brindle boxer barreling toward him at a dead run.

A man and two children were walking in her direction. Cassie's heart almost leaped into her throat it was beating so hard.

Stop it, she thought. It's only a coincidence. Beside her, Max started barking.

When Cassie looked again, she had no idea how she was supposed to sort through her feelings.

"Okay," she told Max. "Go on." She watched him race across the sand and then she started slowly down the steps. Hands in the pockets of her full, denim sundress, she followed the line of Max's footprints down the beach to face the waiting trio.

"You always were way too friendly to anyone who'd slip you a cookie," Cassie muttered.

Despite his sunglasses, there was no doubt who the man was. He waited while she closed the distance between them. Part of her wanted to run away, but the part that held her heart wanted to run straight into his arms.

By the time she'd gotten close enough to greet Nick and the twins, her resolve was back in place. He had hurt her with his lack of trust; she'd be a fool to let him hurt her again.

"Cassie!" Adam exclaimed. "We found you!" Abandoning Max, he and Amanda ran over and threw their arms around her legs.

"Daddy looked and looked," Amanda said, her head tipped back so she could see Cassie's face.

"We waited and waited for you to come back, but you didn't." Adam's voice sounded faintly accusing, even though he was smiling. "You said goodbye to Mandy, but you didn't say it to me."

Cassie put a hand on his curly head. "I know, sweetie, and I'm sorry," she told him. "I had to go away for a while."

Over his head she glared at Nick. "Why did you bring them?" she demanded.

He removed his sunglasses and put them in his pocket. His face was lined with fatigue, but he still looked so dear to her that it was all she could do to keep from throwing herself at him. Her head might know he was bad news, but her heart wasn't listening.

"I brought them to soften you up," he admitted. "Is it working?"

She was tempted to tell him it was. Instead, she forced herself to shake her head. "It just makes things more complicated."

Nick picked up a stick and tossed it as far as he could down the beach. At his command, Max took off running, the twins hot on his heels.

"The situation is simple," Nick contradicted. His shoulders were hunched and his hands were shoved in his pockets as he watched his children play with the dog.

Cassie resisted the urge to ask what he thought the solution was. She was having too difficult a time ignoring the way he looked in his khaki shorts and faded red T-shirt with the words "Bumbershoot Festival" scrawled across the front in faint black script.

His arms and legs were tanned and muscular—a distinct contrast with the shadows beneath his eyes and the lines bracketing his mouth.

Had he lost sleep over her? she wondered. Did his conscience keep him awake?

"The solution," he continued when she didn't ask, "is that you forgive me for being an ignorant, distrustful ass and give me another chance, even though I probably don't deserve one."

"If you don't deserve it, why should I?" she asked.

He turned the full power of his silver gaze on her. "I'm praying you still love me. And I love you more than life."

The plainspoken declaration moved her far more deeply than any flowery speech could have, but still she held back. "Why should I believe you this time? You hurt me before—it could happen again."

"And it probably will," he agreed. "But I'll never hurt you deliberately and I'll never lie to you again. No more tests, I swear, except perhaps another pregnancy test sometime in the future."

Scarcely daring to hope, Cassie pondered his words.

Adam had stopped to investigate something on the ground and Amanda was with him. Max ran around them in a circle, barking.

"Before they come back, there's something I need to tell you," Nick said.

"What is it?"

He sighed and looked away. "The day you told me about the baby, I'd just learned that I wasn't the twins' biological father. I'm afraid I wasn't handling it too well."

"What an awful shock for you!" Cassie exclaimed. She couldn't admit that Bull had already told her. "No wonder you were upset by my news."

"I was for a while, but that's no excuse for the way I acted toward you."

"What are you going to do with them now?" she asked, glancing at the twins, who were slowly making their way back to the cabin.

"Do?" Nick echoed. Comprehension obviously dawned and he smiled. "I talked to an attorney just after you left and he's already been in contact with Janine. She and her count are expecting, so she's willing to give up her rights to the twins—for a slight fee."

"What a terrible woman!" Cassie was horrified.

"They're already mine in every way that matters," Nick said. "I just don't want to take any chances." Nervously, he cleared his throat. "I don't want them to know yet. Time enough for that when they're a little older."

"You're doing the right thing," Cassie told him.

With another glance at the children, he pulled a folded piece of paper from the pocket of his shorts. "I believe in being prepared," he said, "so I took the liberty of preparing a contract. Here."

Startled, Cassie took the paper he thrust at her and unfolded it. This contract appeared to be nearly identical to the one she'd signed when she accepted the job as his nanny. The only things that were different were the job title and the length of time the contract ran.

Cassie read it over slowly as tears began to seep from her eyes. "Oh, Nick."

He stepped closer and then, to her astonishment, he fell to his knees in the sand.

"Please sign. You have no idea how much you mean to me," he declared.

Vaguely, Cassie heard a shout from down the beach. She glanced up to see the twins, followed by Max, running back in their direction.

"Damn," Nick muttered as he got to his feet and brushed the sand from his bare knees. "I was afraid I'd regret bringing them along, but Miles suggested it."

"Miles?" she repeated. "He promised he wouldn't tell."

"He didn't. Not exactly." Nick's grin was lop-sided. "What about it?" he demanded with a gleam in his eye. "Are you going to do the right thing and fulfill that contract?"

Deliberately, Cassie held it up and looked it over again. "'Position, wife,'" she read, voice breaking. "'Length of contract, ninety-nine years.'"

"Will you sign?" Nick asked softly as the kids ran up to them.

"Oh, yes," Cassie replied, heart overflowing with love. "Right on the dotted line."

As Nick bent his head to kiss her, the twins began cheering wildly. "Let's go home and tell Bull," Adam cried. "He'll probably bake us a big cake."

"A chocolate cake," Amanda added.

Epilogue

Six months later

"It's so little and pink!" Adam declared when he, Amanda and Nick came back to Cassie's hospital room from the nursery.

"And it's all wrinkled," Amanda noted. "Like Max."

"The baby's a girl, not an it," Nick reminded them as he sat gingerly on the side of Cassie's bed and took her hand in his. His eyes were lit up with happiness and he was smiling. "Her name's Adele Marie, after your grandmothers."

"Do you like her?" Cassie asked. She was tired, but she couldn't wait for the nurses to bring little Adele back so Cassie could hold her and look her over again.

Between Bull, Nick's mother, Miles, Emma and the twins, Cassie had hardly gotten to hold her at all earlier. Finally, everyone but Nick and the kids had left.

Cassie looked at her little family and her eyes filled with happy tears, as snow began falling outside the window. When he saw her tears, Nick squeezed her hand.

"I love you, Mrs. Kincaid," he whispered as he leaned close.

"I love you, too."

"Oh, they're gonna start that mushy stuff again," Adam groaned. "Let's go back and look at the babies."

Amanda glanced up at Nick. "Our little sister, right?"

Nick smiled at Cassie. Janine had finally signed the papers relinquishing all claims to the twins just the week before.

"That's true," he agreed with Amanda. "I'm your daddy, Adam's daddy and little Adele's daddy, too. With Cassie, we're a family for now and for always."

"Can we go see the babies?" Adam asked.

"Sure." The nursery window was just across the hall. "Stay right there with your sister and don't go anywhere else," Nick told him with mock sternness.

As soon as the twins went out the door, he turned back to Cassie. "I thought they'd never leave."

She giggled at his playful tone and then she sobered. "You're the best daddy in the whole world," she told him.

Nick took her into his arms. "Right now I want to be the best husband I can be."

"The only husband I want," she replied. "And I have a signed contract to prove it." Then she put her arms around Nick's neck and gently tugged until he was close enough to kiss.

For once, the children standing in the doorway didn't interrupt. They just stood quietly, holding hands, and watched.

* * * * * *

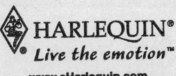

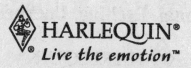

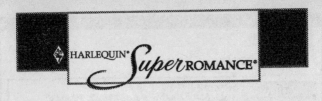

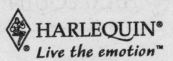

Harlequin Historicals®
Historical Romantic Adventure!

*From rugged lawmen and
valiant knights to defiant heiresses
and spirited frontierswomen,
Harlequin Historicals will
capture your imagination with
their dramatic scope, passion
and adventure.*

*Harlequin Historicals...
they're too good to miss!*

HARLEQUIN®
INTRIGUE®

WE'LL LEAVE YOU BREATHLESS!

If you've been looking for thrilling tales of
contemporary passion and sensuous love stories
with taut, edge-of-the-seat suspense—then
you'll love Harlequin Intrigue!

Every month, you'll meet six new heroes
who are guaranteed to make your spine tingle
and your pulse pound. With them you'll enter
into the exciting world of Harlequin Intrigue—
where your life is on the line
and so is your heart!

THAT'S INTRIGUE—
ROMANTIC SUSPENSE
AT ITS BEST!

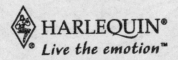

HARLEQUIN®
Live the emotion™

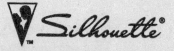